SW

D0358780

HER KNIGHT
IN THE OUTBACK

HER KNIGHT
IN THE OUTBACK

BY

NIKKI LOGAN

First published in Great Britain 2015
by Mills & Boon, an imprint of Harlequin (UK) Limited,
Large Print edition 2015
Eton House, 18-24 Paradise Road,
Richmond, Surrey, TW9 1SR

© 2015 Nikki Logan

ISBN: 978-0-263-25658-1

Harlequin (UK) Limited's policy is to use papers that are natural, renewable and recyclable products and made from wood grown in sustainable forests. The logging and manufacturing processes conform to the legal environmental regulations of the country of origin.

Printed and bound in Great Britain
by CPI Antony Rowe, Chippenham, Wiltshire

For Mat

Acknowledgements

With enormous gratitude to
Dr Richard O'Regan for his help with
the pharmaceutical aspects of this story,
which were integral to its resolution.
And with deepest respect and compassion
for the families of 'The Missing'.

CHAPTER ONE

IT WAS MOMENTS like this that Evelyn Read hated. Life-defining moments. Moments when her fears and prejudices reared up before her eyes and confronted her—just like a King Brown snake, surprised while basking on the hot Australian highway.

She squinted at the distant biker limping carefully towards her out of the shimmering heat mirage and curled her fingers more tightly around the steering wheel.

A moment like this one might have taken her brother. Maybe Trav stopped for the wrong stranger; maybe that was where he went when he disappeared all those months ago. Her instincts screamed that she should press down on her accelerator until the man—the danger—was an hour behind her. But a moment like this might have *saved* her brother, too. If a stranger had only been kind enough or brave enough to stop for him. Then maybe Travis would be back with them right now. Safe. Loved.

Instead of alone, scared…or worse.

The fear of never knowing what happened to him tightened her gut the way it always did when she thought too long about this crazy thing she was doing.

The biker limped closer.

Should she listen to her basest instincts and flee, or respond to twenty-four years of social conditioning and help a fellow human being in trouble? There was probably some kind of outback code to be observed, too, but she'd heard too many stories from too many grieving people to be particularly bothered by niceties.

Eve's eyes flicked to the distant motorbike listing on the side of the long, empty road. And then, closer, to the scruffy man now nearing the restored 1956 Bedford bus that was getting her around Australia.

She glanced at her door's lock to make sure it was secure.

The man limped to a halt next to the bus's bifold doors and looked at her expectantly over his full beard. A dagger tattoo poked out from under his dark T-shirt and impenetrable sunglasses hid his eyes—and his intent—from her.

No. This was her home. She'd never open her front door to a total stranger. Especially not hours from the nearest other people.

She signalled him around to the driver's window instead.

He didn't look too impressed, but he limped his way around to her side and she slid the antique window open and forced her voice to be light.

Sociopaths make a decision on whether you're predator or prey in the first few seconds, she remembered from one of the endless missing-person fact sheets she'd read. She was not about to have 'prey' stamped on her forehead.

'Morning,' she breezed, as if this wasn't potentially a very big deal indeed. 'Looks like you're having a bad day.'

'Emu,' he grunted and she got a glimpse of straight teeth and healthy gums.

Stupidly, that reassured her. As if evil wouldn't floss. She twisted around for evidence of a big damaged bird flailing in the scrub after hitting his motorbike. To validate his claim. 'Was it okay?'

'Yeah, I'm fine, thanks.'

That brought her eyes back to his glasses. 'I can see that. But emus don't always come off the best after a road impact.'

As if she'd know…

'Going that fast, it practically went over the top of me as it ran with its flock. It's probably twenty miles from here now, trying to work out how and when it got black paint on its claws.'

He held up his scratched helmet, which had clearly taken an impact. More evidence. She just nodded, not wanting to give an inch more than necessary. He'd probably already summed her up as a bleeding heart over the emu.

One for the prey column.

'Where are you headed?' he asked.

Her radar flashed again at his interest. 'West.'

Duh, since the Bedford was pointing straight at the sun heading for the horizon and there was nothing else out this way *but* west.

'Can I catch a lift to the closest town?'

Was that tetchiness in his voice because she kept foiling him or because hers was the first vehicle to come along in hours and she was stonewalling him on a ride?

She glanced at his crippled bike.

'That'll have to stay until I can get back here with a truck,' he said, following her glance.

There was something in the sag of his shoulders and the way he spared his injured leg that reassured her even as the beard and tattoo and leather did not. He'd clearly come off his bike hard. Maybe he was more injured than she could see?

But the stark reality was that her converted bus

only had the one seat up front—hers. 'That's my home back there,' she started.

'So...?'

'So, I don't know you.'

Yep. That was absolutely the insult his hardened lips said it was. But she was not letting a stranger back there. Into her world.

'It's only an hour to the border.' He sighed. 'I'll stand on your steps until Eucla.'

Right next to her. Where he could do anything and she couldn't do a thing to avoid it.

'An hour by motorbike, maybe. We take things a little more easy in this old girl. It'll take at least twice that.'

'Fine. I'll stand for two hours, then.'

Or she could just leave him here and send help back. But the image of Trav, lost and in need of help while someone drove off and left him injured and alone, flitted through her mind.

If someone had just been brave...

'I don't know you,' she wavered.

'Look, I get it. A woman travelling alone, big scary biker. You're smart to be cautious but the reality is help might not be able to get to me today so if you leave me here I could be here all night. Freezing my ass off.'

She fumbled for her phone.

His shaggy head shook slightly. 'If we had signal don't you think I'd have used it?'

Sure enough, her phone had diminished to *SOS only*. And as bad as that motorbike looked, it wasn't exactly an emergency.

'Just until we get signal, then?' he pressed, clearly annoyed at having to beg. 'Come on, please?'

How far could that be? They were mostly through the desert now, coming out on the western side of Australia. Where towns and people and telecommunications surely had to exist.

'Have you got some ID?'

He blinked at her and then reached back into his jeans for his wallet.

'No. Not a licence. That could be fake. Got any photos of you?'

He moved slowly, burdened by his incredulity, but pulled his phone out and flicked through a few screens. Then he pressed it up against Eve's window glass.

A serious face looked back at her. Well groomed and in a business shirt. Pretty respectable, really. Almost cute.

Pffff. 'That's not you.'

'Yeah, it is.'

She peered at him again. 'No, it's not.'

It might have been a stock photo off the Internet

for all she knew. The sort of search result she used to get when she googled 'corporate guy' for some design job.

'Oh, for pity's sake...'

He flicked through a few more and found another one, this time more bearded. But nothing like the hairy beast in front of her. Her hesitation obviously spoke volumes so he pushed his sunglasses up onto his head, simultaneously revealing grey eyes and slightly taming his rusty blond hair.

Huh. Okay, maybe it was him.

'Licence?'

A breathed bad word clearly tangled in the long hairs of his moustache but he complied—eventually—and slapped that against the window, too.

Marshall Sullivan.

She held up her phone and took a photo of him through the glass, with his licence in the shot.

'What's that for?'

'Insurance.'

'I just need a lift. That's it. I have no interest in you beyond that.'

'Easy for you to say.'

Her thumbs got busy texting it to both her closest friend and her father in Melbourne. Just to cover bases. Hard to know if the photo would make them more or less confident in this dusty odyssey she was on, but she had to send it to someone.

The grey eyes she could now see rolled. 'We have no signal.'

'The moment we do it will go.'

She hit Send and let the phone slip back down into its little spot on her dash console.

'You have some pretty serious trust issues, lady, you know that?'

'And this is potentially the oldest con in the book. Broken-down vehicle on remote outback road.' She glanced at his helmet and the marks that could be emu claws. 'I'll admit your story has some pretty convincing details—'

'Because it's the truth.'

'—but I'm travelling alone and I'm not going to take any chances. And I'm not letting you in here with me, sorry.' The cab was just too small and risky. 'You'll have to ride in the back.'

'What about all the biker germs I'm going to get all over your stuff?' he grumbled.

'You want a lift or not?'

Those steady eyes glared out at her. 'Yeah. I do.'

And then, as though he couldn't help himself, he grudgingly rattled off a thankyou.

Okay, so it had to be safer to let him loose in the back than have him squished here in the front with her. Her mind whizzed through all the things he might get up to back there but none of them struck her as bad as what he could do up front if he wasn't really who he said he was.

Or even if he was.

Biker boy and his helmet limped back towards the belongings piled on the side of the road next to his disabled bike. Leather jacket, pair of satchels, a box of mystery equipment.

She ground the gears starting the Bedford back up, but rolled up behind him and, as soon as his arms were otherwise occupied with his own stuff, she unlocked the bus and mouthed through the glass of her window. 'Back doors.'

Sullivan limped to the back of the Bedford, lurched it as he climbed in and then slammed himself in there with all her worldly possessions.

Two hours…

'Come on, old chook,' she murmured to the decades-old bus. 'Let's push it a bit, eh?'

Marshall groped around for a light switch but only found a thick fabric curtain. He pulled it back with a swish and light flooded into the darkened interior of the bus. Something extraordinary unfolded in front of him.

He'd seen converted buses before but they were

usually pretty daggy. Kind of worn and soulless and vinyl. But this… This was rich, warm and natural; nothing at all like the hostile lady up front.

It was like a little cottage in some forest. All timber and plush rugs in dark colours. Small, but fully appointed with kitchenette and living space, flat-screen TV, fridge and a sofa. Even potted palms. Compact and long but all there, like one of those twenty-square-metre, fold-down and pull-out apartments they sold in flat packs. At the far end—the driving end—a closed door that must lead to the only absent feature of the vehicle, the bed.

And suddenly he got a sense of Little Miss Hostile's reluctance to let him back here. It was like inviting a total stranger right into your bedroom. Smack bang in the middle of absolutely nowhere.

The bus lurched as she tortured it back up to speed and Marshall stumbled down onto the sofa built into the left side of the vehicle. Not as comfortable as his big eight-seater in the home theatre of his city apartment, but infinitely better than the hard gravel he'd been polishing with his butt for the couple of hours since the bird strike.

Stupid freaking emu. It could have killed them both.

It wasn't as if a KTM 1190 was a stealth unit but maybe, at the speed the emu had been going, the air rushing past its ears was just as noisy as an approaching motorbike. And then their fates had collided. Literally.

He sagged down against the sofa back and resisted the inclination to examine his left foot. Sometimes boots were the only things that kept fractured bones together after bike accidents so he wasn't keen to take it off unless he was bleeding to death. In fact, particularly if he was bleeding to death because something told him the hostess-with-the-leastest would not be pleased if he bled out all over her timber floor. But he could at least elevate it. That was generally good for what ailed you. He dragged one of his satchels up onto the sofa, turned and stacked a couple of the bouncy, full pillows down the opposite end and then swung his abused limb up onto it, lying out the full length of the sofa.

'Oh, yeah...' Half words, half groan. All good.

He loved his bike. He loved the speed. He loved that direct relationship with the country you had when there was no car between you and it. And he loved the freedom from everything he'd found touring that country.

But he really didn't love how fragile he'd turned out to be when something went wrong at high speed.

As stacks went, it had been pretty controlled. Especially considering the fishtail he'd gone into as the mob of emu shot past and around him. But even a controlled slide hurt—him and the bike—and once the adrenaline wore off and the birds disappeared over the dusty horizon, all he'd been left with was the desert silence and the pain.

And no phone signal.

Normally that wouldn't bother him. There really couldn't be enough alone time in this massive country, as far as he was concerned. If you travelled at the right time of year—and that would be the *wrong* time of year for tourists—you could pretty much have most outback roads to yourself. He was free to do whatever he wanted, wear whatever he wanted, be as hairy as he wanted, shower whenever he wanted. Or not. He'd given up caring what people thought of him right about the time he'd stopped caring about people.

Ancient history.

And life was just simpler that way.

The stoic old Bedford finally shifted into top gear and the rattle of its reconditioned engine evened out to a steady hum, vibrating under his skin as steadily as his bike did. He took the rare opportunity to do what he could never do when at the controls: he closed his eyes and let the hum take him.

Two hours, she'd said. He could be up on his feet with her little home fully restored before she even

made it from the front of the bus back to the rear
doors. As if no one had ever been there.

Two hours to rest. Recover. And enjoy the roads
he loved from a more horizontal perspective.

'Who's been sleeping in my bed?' Eve muttered as
she stood looking at the bear of a man fast asleep
on her little sofa.

What was this—some kind of reverse Goldilocks
thing?

She cleared her throat. Nothing. He didn't even
shift in his sleep.

'Mr Sullivan?'

Nada.

For the first time, it occurred to her that maybe
this wasn't sleep; maybe this was coma. Maybe he'd
been injured more than either of them had realised.
She hauled herself up into the back of the bus and
crossed straight to his side, all thoughts of dangerous tattooed men cast aside. Her fingertips brushed
below the hairy tangle of his jaw.

Steady and strong. And warm.

Phew.

'Mr Sullivan,' she said, louder. Those dark blond
brows twitched just slightly and something moved
briefly behind his eyelids, so she pressed her advantage. 'We're here.'

Her gaze went to his elevated foot and then back up to where his hands lay, folded, across the T-shirt over his midsection. Rather nice hands. Soft and manicured despite the patches of bike grease from his on-road repairs.

The sort of hands you'd see in a magazine.

Which was ridiculous. How many members of motorcycle clubs sidelined in a bit of casual hand modelling?

She forced her focus back up to his face and opened her lips to call his name a little louder, but, where before there was only the barest movement behind his lids, now they were wide open and staring straight at her. This close, with the light streaming in from the open curtains, she saw they weren't grey at all—or not *just* grey, at least. The pewter irises were flecked with rust that neatly matched the tarnished blond of his hair and beard, particularly concentrated around his pupils.

She'd never seen eyes like them. She immediately thought of the burnt umber coastal rocks of the far north, where they slid down to pale, clean ocean. And where she'd started her journey eight months ago.

'We're here,' she said, irritated at her own breathlessness. And at being caught checking him out.

He didn't move, but maybe that was because she

was leaning so awkwardly over him from all the pulse-taking.

'Where's here?' he croaked.

She pushed back onto her heels and dragged her hands back from the heat of his body. 'The border. You'll have to get up while they inspect the bus.'

They took border security seriously here on the invisible line between South Australia and Western Australia. Less about gun-running and drug-trafficking and more about fruit flies and honey. Quarantine was king when agriculture was your primary industry.

Sullivan twisted gingerly into an upright position, then carefully pulled himself to his feet and did his best to put the cushions back where they'd started. Not right, but he got points for the effort.

So he hadn't been raised by leather-clad wolves, then.

He bundled up his belongings, tossed them to the ground outside the bus and lowered himself carefully down.

'How is your leg?' Eve asked.

'I'll live.'

Okay. Man of few words. Clearly, he'd spent too much time in his own company.

The inspection team made quick work of hunting over every inch of her converted bus and Sullivan's saddlebags. She'd become proficient at dumping or eating anything that was likely to get picked up at the border and so, this time, the team only found one item to protest—a couple of walnuts not yet consumed.

Into the bin they went.

She lifted her eyes towards Sullivan, deep in discussion with one of the border staff who had him in one ear and their phone on the other. Arranging assistance for his crippled bike, presumably. As soon as they were done, he limped back towards her and hiked his bags up over his shoulder.

'Thanks for the ride,' he said as though the effort half choked him.

'You don't need to go into Eucla?' Just as she'd grown used to him.

'They're sending someone out to grab me and retrieve my bike.'

'Oh. Great that they can do it straight away.'

'Country courtesy.'

As opposed to her lack of...? 'Well, good luck with your—'

It was then she realised she had absolutely no idea what he was doing out here, other than hitting random emus. In all her angsting out on the deserted highway, she really hadn't stopped to wonder, let alone ask.

'—with your travels.'

His nod was brisk and businesslike. 'Cheers.'

And then he was gone, back towards the border security office and the little café that catered for people delayed while crossing. Marshall Sullivan didn't seem half so scary here in a bustling border stop, though his beard was no less bushy and the ink dagger under his skin no less menacing. All the what-ifs she'd felt two hours ago on that long empty road hobbled away from her as he did.

And she wondered how she'd possibly missed the first time how well his riding leathers fitted him.

CHAPTER TWO

IT WAS THE raised voices that first got Marshall's attention. Female, anxious and angry, almost swallowed up by drunk, male and belligerent.

'Stop!'

The fact a gaggle of passers-by had formed a wide, unconscious circle around the spectacle in the middle of town was the only reason he sauntered closer instead of running on his nearly healed leg. If something bad was happening, he had to assume someone in the handful of people assembled would have intervened. Or at least cried out. Him busting in to an unknown situation, half-cocked, was no way to defuse what was clearly an escalating situation.

Instead, he insinuated himself neatly into the heart of the onlookers and nudged his way through to the front until he could get his eyeballs on things. A flutter of paper pieces rained down around them as the biggest of the men tore something up.

'You put another one up, I'm just going to rip it down,' he sneered.

The next thing he saw was the back of a woman's head. Dark, travel-messy ponytail. Dwarfed by the men she was facing but not backing down.

And all too familiar.

Little Miss Hostile. Winning friends and influencing people—as usual.

'This is a public noticeboard,' she asserted up at the human mountain, foolishly undeterred by his size.

'For Norseman residents,' he spat. 'Not for blow-ins from the east.'

'Public,' she challenged. 'Do I need to spell it out for you?'

Wow. Someone really needed to give her some basic training in conflict resolution. The guy was clearly a xenophobe and drunk. Calling him stupid in front of a crowd full of locals wasn't the fastest way out of her predicament.

She shoved past him and used a staple gun to pin up another flier.

He'd seen the same poster peppering posts and walls in Madura, Cocklebiddy and Balladonia. Every point along the remote desert highway that could conceivably hold a person. And a sign. Crisp and new against all the bleached, frayed ones from years past.

'Stop!'

Yeah, that guy wasn't going to stop. And now the McTanked Twins were also getting in on the act.

Goddammit.

Marshall pushed out into the centre of the circle. He raised his voice the way he used to in office meetings when they became unruly. Calm but intractable. 'Okay, show's over, people.'

The crowd turned their attention to him, like a bunch of cattle. So did the three drunks. But they weren't so intoxicated they didn't pause at the sight of his beard and tattoos. Just for a moment.

The moment he needed.

'Howzabout we find somewhere else for those?' he suggested straight to Little Miss Hostile, neatly relieving her of the pile of posters with one hand and the staple gun with his other. 'There are probably better locations in town.'

She spun around and glared at him in the heartbeat before she recognised him. 'Give me those.'

He ignored her and spoke to the crowd. 'All done, people. Let's get moving.'

They parted for him as he pushed back through, his hands full of her property. She had little choice but to pursue him.

'Those are mine!'

'Let's have this conversation around the corner,' he gritted back and down towards her.

But just as they'd cleared the crowd, the big guy couldn't help himself.

'Maybe he's gone missing to get away from you!' he called.

A shocked gasp covered the sound of small female feet pivoting on the pavement and she marched straight back towards the jeering threesome.

Marshall shoved the papers under his arm and sprinted after her, catching her just before she re-entered the eye of the storm. All three men had lined up in it, ready. Eager. He curled his arms around her and dragged her back, off her feet, and barked just one word in her ear.

'Don't!'

She twisted and lurched and swore the whole way but he didn't loosen his hold until the crowd and the jeering laughter of the drunks were well behind them.

'Put me down,' she struggled. 'Ass!'

'The only ass around here is the one I just saved.'

'I've dealt with rednecks before.'

'Yeah, you were doing a bang-up job.'

'I have every right to put my posters up.'

'No argument. But you could have just walked away and then come back and done it in ten minutes when the drunks were gone.'

'But there were thirty people there.'

'None of whom were making much of an effort to help you.' In case she hadn't noticed.

'I didn't want their help,' she spat, spinning back to face him. 'I wanted their attention.'

What was this—some kind of performance art thing? 'Come again?'

'Thirty people would have read my poster, remembered it. The same people that probably would have passed it by without noticing, otherwise.'

'Are you serious?'

She snatched the papers and staple gun back from him and clutched them to her heaving chest. 'Perfectly. You think I'm new to this?'

'I really don't know what to think. You treated me like a pariah because of a bit of leather and ink, but you were quite happy to face off against the Beer Gut Brothers, back there.'

'It got *attention*.'

'So does armed robbery. Are you telling me the bank is on your to-do list in town?'

She glared at him. 'You don't understand.'

And then he was looking at the back of her head again as she turned and marched away from him without so much as a goodbye. Let alone a thankyou.

He cursed under his breath.

'Enlighten me,' he said, catching up with her and ignoring the protest of his aching leg.

'Why should I?'

'Because I just risked my neck entering that fray to help you and that means you owe me one.'

'I rescued you out on the highway. I'd say that makes us even.'

Infuriating woman. He slammed on the brakes. 'Fine. Whatever.'

Her momentum carried her a few metres further but then she spun back. 'Did you look at the poster?'

'I've been looking at them since the border.'

'And?'

'And what?'

'What's on it?'

His brows forked. What the hell *was* on it? 'Guy's face. Bunch of words.' And a particularly big one in red. MISSING. 'It's a missing-person poster.'

'Bingo. And you've been looking at them since the border but can't tell me what he looked like or what his name was or what it was about.' She took two steps closer. 'That's why getting their attention was so valuable.'

Realisation washed through him and he felt like a schmuck for parachuting in and rescuing her like some damsel in distress. 'Because they'll remember it. You.'

'Him!' But her anger didn't last long. It seemed to

desert her like the adrenaline in both their bodies, leaving her flat and exhausted. 'Maybe.'

'What do you do—start a fight in every town you go to?'

'Whatever it takes.'

Cars went by with stereos thumping.

'Listen…' Suddenly, Little Miss Hostile had all new layers. And most of them were laden with sadness. 'I'm sorry if you had that under control. Where I come from you don't walk past a woman crying out in the street.'

Actually, that wasn't strictly true because he came from a pretty rough area and sometimes the best thing to do was keep walking. But while his mother might have raised her kids like that, his grandparents certainly hadn't. And he, at least, had learned from their example even if his brother, Rick, hadn't.

Dark eyes studied him. 'That must get you into a lot of trouble,' she eventually said.

True enough.

'Let me buy you a drink. Give those guys some time to clear out and then I'll help you put the posters up.'

'I don't need your help. Or your protection.'

'Okay, but I'd like to take a proper look at that poster.'

He regarded her steadily as uncertainty flooded

her expression. The same that he'd seen out on the highway. 'Or is the leather still bothering you?'

Indecision flooded her face and her eyes flicked from his beard to his eyes, then down to his lips and back again.

'No. You haven't robbed or murdered me yet. I think a few minutes together in a public place will be fine.'

She turned and glanced down the street where a slight *doof-doof* issued from an architecturally classic Aussie hotel. Then her voice filled with warning. 'Just one.'

It was hard not to smile. Her stern little face was like a daisy facing up to a cyclone.

'If I was going to hurt you I've had plenty of opportunity. I don't really need to get you liquored up.'

'Encouraging start to the conversation.'

'You know my name,' he said, moving his feet in a pubward direction. 'I don't know yours.'

She regarded him steadily. Then stuck out the hand with the staple gun clutched in it. 'Evelyn Read. Eve.'

He shook half her hand and half the tool. 'What do you like to drink, Eve?'

'I don't. Not in public. But you go ahead.'

A teetotaller in an outback pub.

Well, this should be fun.

* * *

Eve trusted Marshall Sullivan with her posters while she used the facilities. When she came back, he'd smoothed out all the crinkles in the top one and was studying it.

'Brother?' he said as she slid into her seat.

'What makes you say that?'

He tapped the surname on the poster where it had *Travis James Read* in big letters.

'He could be my husband.' She shrugged.

His eyes narrowed. 'Same dark hair. Same shape eyes. He looks like you.'

Yeah, he did. Everyone thought so. 'Trav is my little brother.'

'And he's missing?'

God, she hated this bit. The pity. The automatic assumption that something bad had happened. Hard enough not letting herself think it every single day without having the thought planted back in her mind by strangers at every turn.

Virtual strangers.

Though, at least this one did her the courtesy of not referring to Travis in the past tense. Points for that.

'Missing a year next week, actually.'

'Tough anniversary. Is that why you're out here? Is this where he was last seen?'

She lifted her gaze back to his. 'No. In Melbourne.'

'So what brings you out west?'

'I ran out of towns on the east coast.'

Blond brows lowered. 'You've lost me.'

'I'm visiting every town in the country. Looking for him. Putting up notices. Doing the legwork.'

'I assumed you were just on holidays or something.'

'No. This is my job.'

Now. Before that she'd been a pretty decent graphic designer for a pretty decent marketing firm. Until she'd handed in her notice.

'Putting up posters is your job?'

'Finding my brother.' The old defensiveness washed through her. 'Is anything more important?'

His confusion wasn't new. He wasn't the first person not to understand what she was doing. By far. Her own father didn't even get it; he just wanted to grieve Travis's absence as though he were dead. To accept he was gone.

She was light-years and half a country away from being ready to accept such a thing. She and Trav had been so close. If he was dead, wouldn't she feel it?

'So…what, you just drive every highway in the country pinning up notices?'

'Pretty much. Trying to trigger a memory in someone's mind.'

'And it's taken you a year to do the east coast?'

'About eight months. Though I started up north.'
And that was where she'd finish.

'What happened before that?'

Guilt hammered low in her gut for those missing couple of months before she'd realised how things really were. How she'd played nice and sat on her hands while the police seemed to achieve less and less. Maybe if she'd started sooner—

'I trusted the system.'

'But the authorities didn't find him?'

'There are tens of thousands of missing people every year. I just figured that the only people who could make Trav priority number one were his family.'

'That many? Really?'

'Teens. Kids. Women. Most are located pretty quickly.'

But ten per cent weren't.

His eyes tracked down to the birthdate on the poster. 'Healthy eighteen-year-old males don't really make it high up the priority list?'

A small fist formed in her throat. 'Not when there's no immediate evidence of foul play.'

And even if they maybe weren't entirely healthy, psychologically. But Travis's depression was hardly unique amongst *The Missing* and his anxiety attacks were longstanding enough that the authorities dismissed them as irrelevant. As if a bathroom cabinet awash with mental health medicines wasn't relevant.

A young woman with bright pink hair badly in need of a recolour brought Marshall's beer and Eve's lime and bittes and sloshed them on the table.

'That explains the bus,' he said. 'It's very…homey.'

'It is my home. Mine went to pay for the trip.'

'You sold your house?'

Her chin kicked up. 'And resigned from my job. I can't afford to be distracted by having to earn an income while I cover the country.'

She waited for the inevitable judgment.

'That's quite a commitment. But it makes sense.'

Such unconditional acceptance threw her. Everyone else she'd told thought she was foolish. Or plain crazy. Implication: like her brother. No one just… nodded.

'That's it? No opinion? No words of wisdom?'

His eyes lifted to hers. 'You're a grown woman. You did what you needed to do. And I assume it was your asset to dispose of.'

She scrutinised him again. The healthy, unmarked skin under the shaggy beard. The bright eyes. The even teeth.

'What's your story?' she asked.

'No story. I'm travelling.'

'You're not a bikie.' Statement, not question.

'Not everyone with a motorbike belongs in an out-law club,' he pointed out.

'You look like a bikie.'

'I wear leather because it's safest when you get too intimate with asphalt. I have a beard because one of the greatest joys in life is not having to shave, and so I indulge that when I'm travelling alone.'

She glanced down to where the dagger protruded from his T-shirt sleeve. 'And the tattoo?'

His eyes immediately darkened. 'We were all young and impetuous once.'

'Who's Christine?'

'Christine's not relevant to this discussion.'

Bang. Total shutdown. 'Come on, Marshall. I aired my skeleton.'

'Something tells me you air it regularly. To any-one who'll listen.'

Okay, this time the criticism was unmistakable. She pushed more upright in her chair. 'You were asking the questions, if you recall.'

'Don't get all huffy. We barely know each other. Why would I spill my guts to a stranger?'

'I don't know. Why would you rescue a stranger on the street?'

'Not wanting to see you beaten to a pulp and not

wanting to share my dirty laundry are very different things.'

'Oh, Christine's dirty laundry?'

His lips thinned even further and he pushed away from the table. 'Thanks for the drink. Good luck with your brother.'

She shot to her feet, too. 'Wait. Marshall?'

He stopped and turned back slowly.

'I'm sorry. I guess I'm out of practice with people,' she said.

'You're not kidding.'

'Where are you staying?'

'In town.'

Nice and non-specific. 'I'm a bit... I get a bit tired of eating in the bus. On my own. Can I interest you in something to eat, later?'

'I don't think so.'

Walk away, Eve. That would be the smart thing to do.

'I'll change the subject. Not my brother. Not your...' *Not your Christine?* 'We can talk about places we've been. Favourite sights.' Her voice petered out.

His eyebrows folded down over his eyes briefly and disguised them from her view. But he finally relented. 'There's a café across the street from my motel. End of this road.'

'Sounds good.'

She didn't usually eat out, to save money, but then she didn't usually have the slightest hint of company either. One dinner wouldn't kill her. Alone with a stranger. Across the road from his motel room.

'It's not a date, though,' she hastened to add.

'No.' The moustache twisted up on the left. 'It's not.'

And as he and his leather pants sauntered back out of the bar, she felt like an idiot. An adolescent idiot. *Of course* this was not a date and *of course* he wouldn't have considered it such. Hairy, lone-wolf types who travelled the country on motorbikes probably didn't stand much on ceremony when it came to women. Or bother with dates.

She'd only mentioned a meal at all because she felt bad that she'd pressed an obvious sore point with him after he'd shown her nothing but interest and acceptance about Travis.

facepalm

Her brother's favourite saying flittered through her memory and never seemed more appropriate. Hopefully, a few hours and a good shower from now she could be a little more socially appropriate and a lot less hormonal.

Inexplicably so.

Unwashed biker types were definitely not her

thing, no matter how nice their smiles. Normally, the *eau de sweaty man* that littered towns in the Australian bush flared her nostrils. But as Marshall Sullivan had hoisted her up against his body out in the street she'd definitely responded to the powerful circle of his hold, the hard heat of his chest and the warmth of his hissed words against her ear.

Even though it came with the tickle of his substantial beard against her skin.

She was *so* not a beard woman.

A man who travelled the country alone was almost certainly doing it for a reason. Running from something or someone. Dropping out of society. Hiding from the authorities. Any number of mysterious and dangerous things.

Or maybe Marshall Sullivan was just as socially challenged as she was.

Maybe that was why she had a sudden and unfathomable desire to sit across a table from the man again.

'See you at seven-thirty, then,' she called after him.

Eve's annoyance at herself for being late—and at caring about that—turned into annoyance at Marshall Sullivan for being even later. What, had he got lost crossing the street?

Her gaze scanned the little café diner as she entered—over the elderly couple with a stumpy candle, past the just-showered Nigel No Friends reading a book and the two men arguing over the sports pages. But as her eyes grazed back around to the service counter, they stumbled over the hands wrapped around *Nigel*'s battered novel. Beautiful hands.

She stepped closer. 'Marshall?'

Rust-flecked eyes glanced up to her. And then he pushed to his feet. To say he was a changed man without the beard would have been an understatement. He was transformed. His hair hadn't been cut but it was slicked back either with product or he truly had just showered. But his face…

Free of the overgrown blondish beard and moustache, his eyes totally stole focus, followed only by his smooth broad forehead. She'd always liked an unsullied forehead. Reliable somehow.

He slid a serviette into the book to mark his place and closed it.

She glanced at the cover. *'Gulliver's Travels?'*

Though what she really wanted to say was… *You shaved?*

'I carry a few favourites around with me in my pack.'

She slid in opposite him, completely unable to take her eyes off his new face. At a loss to reconcile it as the under layer of all that sweat, dust and helmet hair she'd encountered out on the road just a few days ago. 'What makes it a favourite?'

He thought about that for a bit. 'The journeying. It's very human. And Gulliver is a constant reminder that perspective is everything in life.'

Huh. She'd just enjoyed it for all the little people. They fell to silence.

'You shaved,' she finally blurted.

'I did.'

'For dinner?' Dinner that wasn't a date.

His neatly groomed head shook gently. 'I do that periodically. Take it off and start again. Even symbols of liberty need maintenance.'

'That's what it means to you? Freedom?'

'Isn't that what the Bedford means to you?'

Freedom? No. Sanity, yes. 'The bus is just transport and accommodation conveniently bundled.'

'You forget I've seen inside it. That's not convenience. That's sanctuary.'

Yeah…it was, really. But she didn't know him well enough to open up to that degree.

'I bought the Bedford off this old carpenter after his wife died. He couldn't face travelling any more without her.'

'I wonder if he knows what he's missing.'

'Didn't you just say perspective was everything?'

'True enough.'

A middle-aged waitress came bustling over, puffing, as though six people at once was the most she'd seen in a week. She took their orders from the limited menu and bustled off again.

One blond brow lifted. 'You carb-loading for a marathon?'

'You've seen the stove in the Bedford. I can only cook the basics in her. Every now and again I like to take advantage of a commercial kitchen's deep-fryer.'

Plus, boiling oil would kill anything that might otherwise not get past the health code. There was nothing worse than being stuck in a small town, throwing your guts up. Unless it was being stuck on the side of the road between small towns and kneeling in the roadside gravel.

'So, you know how I'm funding my way around the country,' she said. 'How are you doing it?'

He stared at her steadily. 'Guns and drugs.'

'Ha-ha.'

'That's what you thought when you saw me. Right?'

'I saw a big guy on a lonely road trying really hard to get into my vehicle. What would you have done?'

Those intriguing eyes narrowed just slightly but

then flicked away. 'I'm out here working. Like you. Going from district to district.'

'Working for who?'

'Federal Government.'

'Ooh, the Feds. That sounds much more exciting than it probably is. What department?'

He took a long swig of his beer before answering. 'Meteorology.'

She stared. 'You're a *weatherman*?'

'Right. I stand in front of a green screen every night and read maximums and minimums.'

Her smile broadened. 'You're a weatherman.'

He sagged back in his chair and spoke as if he'd heard this one time too many. 'Meteorology is a science.'

'You don't look like a scientist.' Definitely not before and, even clean shaven, Marshall was still too muscular and tattooed.

'Would it help if I was in a lab coat and glasses?'

'Yes.' Because the way he packed out his black T-shirt was the least nerdy thing she'd ever seen. 'So why are my taxes funding your trip around the country, exactly?'

'You're not earning. You don't pay taxes.'

The man had a point. 'Why are you out here, then?'

'I'm auditing the weather stations. I check them, report on their condition.'

Well, that explained the hands. 'I thought you were this free spirit on two wheels. You're an auditor.'

His lips tightened. 'Something tells me that's a step down from weatherman in your eyes.'

She got stuck into her complimentary bread roll, buttering and biting into it. 'How many stations are there?'

'Eight hundred and ninety-two.'

'And they send one man?' Surely they had locals that could check to make sure possums hadn't moved into their million-dollar infrastructure.

'I volunteered to do the whole run. Needed the break.'

From...? But she'd promised not to ask. They were supposed to be talking about travel highlights. 'Where was the most remote station?'

'Giles. Seven hundred and fifty clicks west of Alice. Up in the Gibson Desert.'

Alice Springs. Right smack bang in the middle of their massive island continent. 'Where did you start?'

'Start and finish in Perth.'

A day and a half straight drive from here. 'Is Perth home?'

'Sydney.'

She visualised the route he must have taken clockwise around the country from the west. 'So you're nearly done, then?'

His laugh drew the eyes of the other diners. 'Yeah. If two-thirds of the weather stations weren't in the bottom third of the state.'

'Do you get to look around? Or is it all work?'

He shrugged. 'Some places I skip right through. Others I linger. I have some flexibility.'

Eve knew exactly what that was like. Some towns whispered to you like a lover. Others yelled at you to go. She tended to move on quickly from those.

'Favourites so far?'

And he was off… Talking about the places that had captivated him most. The prehistoric, ferny depths of the Claustral Canyon, cave-diving in the crystal-clear ponds on South Australia's limestone coast, the soul-restoring solidity of Katherine Gorge in Australia's north.

'And the run over here goes without saying.'

'The Nullabor?' Pretty striking with its epic treeless stretches of desert but not the most memorable place she could recall.

'The Great Australian Bight,' he clarified.

She just blinked at him.

'You got off the highway on the way over, right? Turned for the coast?'

'My focus is town to town.'

He practically gaped. 'One of the most spectacular natural wonders in the world was just a half-hour drive away.'

'And half an hour back. That was an hour sooner I could have made it to the next town.'

His brows dipped over grey eyes. 'You've got to get out more.'

'I'm on the job.'

'Yeah, me, too, but you have to live as well. What about weekends?'

The criticism rankled. 'Not all of us are on the cushy public servant schedule. An hour—a day— could mean the difference between running across someone who knew Travis and not.'

Or even running into Trav himself.

'What if they came through an hour after you left, and pausing to look at something pretty could have meant your paths crossed?'

Did he think she hadn't tortured herself with those thoughts late at night? The endless what-ifs?

'An hour afterwards and they'll see a poster. An hour before and they'd have no idea their shift buddy is a missing person.' At least that was what she told herself. Sternly.

Marshall blinked at her.

'You don't understand.' How could he?

'Wouldn't it be faster to just email the posters around the country? Ask the post offices to put them up for you.'

'It's not just about the posters. It's about talking to people. Hunting down leads. Making an impression.'

Hoping to God the impression would stick.

'The kind you nearly made this afternoon?'

'Whatever it takes.'

Their meals arrived and the next minute was filled with making space on the table and receiving their drinks.

'Anyway, weren't we supposed to be talking about something else?' Eve said brightly, crunching into a chip. 'Where are you headed next?'

'Up to Kalgoorlie, then Southern Cross.'

North. Complete opposite to her.

'You?' His gaze was neutral enough.

'Esperance. Ravensthorpe. With a side trip out to Israelite Bay.' Jeez—why didn't she just draw him her route on a serviette? 'I'm getting low on posters after the Nullabor run. Need an MP's office.'

His newly groomed head tipped.

'MP's offices are obliged by law to print missing-person posters on request,' she explained. 'And there's one in Esperance.'

'Convenient.'

She glared at her chicken. 'It's the least they could do.'

And pretty much all they did. Though they were usually carefully sympathetic.

'It must be hard,' he murmured between mouthfuls. 'Hitting brick walls everywhere you go.'

'I'd rather hit them out here than stuck back in Melbourne. At least I can be productive here.'

Sitting at home and relying on others to do something to find her brother had nearly killed her.

'Did you leave a big family behind?'

Instantly her mind flashed to her father's grief-stricken face as the only person he had left in the world drove off towards the horizon. 'Just my dad.'

'No mum?'

She sat up straighter in her seat. If Christine-of-the-dagger was off the table for discussion, her drunk mother certainly was. Clearly, the lines in her face were as good as a barometric map. Because Marshall let the subject well and truly drop.

'Well, guess this is our first and last dinner, then,' he said cheerfully, toasting her with a forkful of mashed potato and peas. There was nothing more in that than pure observation. Nothing enough that she felt confident in answering without worrying it would sound like an invitation.

'You never know, we might bump into each other again.'

But, really, how likely was that once they headed off towards opposite points on the compass? The only reason they'd met up this once was because there was only one road in and out of the south half of this vast state and he'd crashed into an emu right in the middle of it.

Thoughtful eyes studied her face, then turned back to his meal.

'So you're not from Sydney, originally?'

Marshall pushed his empty plate away and groaned inwardly. Who knew talking about nothing could be so tiring? This had to be the greatest number of words he'd spoken to anyone in weeks. But it was his fault as much as hers. No dagger tattoo and no missing brother. That was what he'd stipulated. She'd held up her end of the bargain, even though she was clearly itching to know more.

Precisely why he didn't do dinners with women.

Conversation.

He'd much rather get straight to the sex part. Although that was clearly off the table with Eve. So it really made a man wonder why the heck he'd said yes to Eve's 'not a date' invitation. Maybe even *he* got lonely.

And maybe they were now wearing long coats in Hades.

'Brisbane.'

'How old were you when you moved?' she chatted on, oblivious to the rapid congealing of his thoughts. Oblivious to the dangerous territory she'd accidentally stumbled into. Thoughts of his brother, their mother and how tough he'd found Sydney as an adolescent.

'Twelve.'

The word squeezed past his suddenly tight throat. The logical part of him knew it was just polite conversation, but the part of him that was suddenly as taut as a crossbow loaded a whole lot more onto her innocent chatter. Twelve was a crap age to be yanked away from your friends and the school where you were finding your feet and thrust into one of the poorest suburbs of one of the biggest cities in the country. But—for the woman who'd only pumped out a second son for the public benefits—moving states to chase a more generous single-parent allowance was a no-brainer. No matter who it disrupted.

Not that any of that money had ever found its way to him and Rick. They were just a means to an end.

'What was that like?'

Being your mother's meal ticket or watching your

older brother forge himself a career as the local drug-mover?

'It was okay.'

Uh-oh…here it came. Verbal shutdown. Probably just as well, given the direction his mind was going.

She watched him steadily, those dark eyes knowing something was up even if she didn't know exactly what. 'Uh-huh…'

Which was code for *Your turn next, Oscar Wilde.* But he couldn't think of a single thing to say, witty or otherwise. So he folded his serviette and gave his chair the slightest of backward pushes.

'Well…'

'What just happened?' Eve asked, watching him with curiosity but not judgment. And not moving an inch.

'It's getting late.'

'It's eight-thirty.'

Seriously? Only an hour? It felt like eternity.

'I'm heading out at sunrise. So I can get to Lake Lefroy before it gets too hot.'

And back to blissful isolation, where he didn't need to explain himself to anyone.

She tipped her head and it caused her dark hair to swing to the right a little. A soft fragrance wafted forwards and teased his receptors. His words stumbled as surely as he did, getting up. 'Thanks for the company.'

She followed suit. 'You're welcome.'

They split the bill in uncomfortable silence, then stepped out into the dark street. Deserted by eight-thirty.

Eve looked to her right, then back at him.

'Listen, I know you're just across the road but could you...would you mind walking me back to the bus?'

Maybe they were both remembering those three jerks from earlier.

'Where do you park at night?' He suddenly realised he had no idea where she'd pulled up. And that his ability to form sentences seemed to have returned with the fresh air.

'I usually find a good spot...'

Oh, jeez. She wasn't even sorted for the night.

They walked on in silence and then words just came tumbling out of him.

'My motel booking comes with parking. You could use that if you want. I'll tuck the bike forward.'

'Really?' Gratitude flooded her pretty face. 'That would be great, thank you.'

'Come on.'

He followed her to the right, and walked back through Norseman's quiet main streets. Neither of

them spoke. When they reached her bus, she unlocked the side window and reached in to activate
the folding front door. He waited while she crossed
back around and then stepped up behind her into
the cab.

Forbidden territory previously.

But she didn't so much as twitch this time. Which
was irrationally pleasing. Clearly he'd passed some
kind of test. Maybe it was when the beard came off.

The Bedford rumbled to life and Eve circled the
block before heading back to his motel. He directed
her into his bay and then jumped out to nudge the
KTM forward a little. The back of her bus stuck out
of the bay but he was pretty sure there was only one
other person in the entire motel and they were already parked up for the night.

'Thanks again for this,' she said, pausing at the
back of the bus with one of the two big rear doors
open.

Courtesy of the garish motel lights that streamed
in her half-closed curtains, he could see the comfortable space he'd fallen asleep in bathed in a yellow
glow. And beyond it, behind the door that now stood
open at the other end of the bus, Eve's bedroom. The
opening was dominated by the foot of a large mat-
tress draped in a burgundy quilt and weighed down
with two big cushions.

Nothing like the sterile motel room and single country bed he'd be returning to.

'Caravan parks can be a little isolated this time of year,' she said, a bit tighter, as she caught the direction of his gaze. 'I feel better being close to... people.'

He eased his shoulder against the closed half of the door and studied her. Had she changed her mind? Was that open door some kind of unconscious overture? And was he really considering taking her up on it if it was? Pretty, uptight girls on crusades didn't really meet his definition of uncomplicated. Yet something deep inside hinted strongly that she might be worth a bit of complication.

He peered down on her in the shadows. 'No problem.'

She shuffled from left foot to right. 'Well...'night, then. See you in the morning. Thanks again.'

A reluctant smile crossed his face at the firm finality of that door slamming shut. And at the zipping across of curtains as he sauntered to the rear of the motel.

Now they were one-for-one in the inappropriate social reaction stakes. He'd gone all strong and silent on her and she'd gone all blushing virgin on him.

Equally awkward.

Equally regrettable.

He dug into his pocket for the worn old key and let himself into his ground floor room. Exactly as soulless and bland as her little bus wasn't.

But exactly as soulless and bland as he preferred.

CHAPTER THREE

'THIS BUS NEVER stops being versatile, does it?'

Eve's breath caught deep in her throat at the slight twang and comfortable gravel in the voice that came from her left. The few days that had passed since she'd heard his bike rumble out of the motel car park at dawn as she'd rolled the covers more tightly around her and fell back to sleep gave him exactly the right amount of stubble as he let the beard grow back in.

'Marshall?' Her hand clamped down on the pile of fliers that lifted off the table in the brisk Esperance waterfront breeze. 'I thought you'd headed north?'

'I did. But a road train had jack-knifed across the highway just out of Kal and the spill clean-up was going to take twenty-four hours so I adjusted my route. I'll do the south-west anti-clockwise. Like you.'

Was there just the slightest pause before 'like you'? And did that mean anything? Apparently, she took too long wondering because he started up again.

'I assumed I'd have missed you, actually.'

Or hoped? Impossible to know with his eyes hidden behind seriously dark sunglasses. Still, if he'd truly wanted to avoid her he could have just kept walking just now. She was so busy promoting *The Missing* to locals she never would have noticed him.

Eve pushed her shoulders back to improve her posture, which had slumped as the morning wore on. Convenient coincidence that it also made the best of her limited assets.

'I had to do Salmon Gums and Gibson on the way,' she said. 'I only arrived last night.'

He took in the two-dozen posters affixed to the tilted up doors of the bus's luggage compartment. It made a great roadside noticeboard to set her fold-out table up in front of.

He strolled up and back, studying every face closely.

'Who are all these people?'

'They're all long-termers.' *The ten per cent.*

'Do you know them all?'

'No,' she murmured. 'But I know most of their families. Online, at least.'

'All missing.' He frowned. 'Doesn't it pull focus from your brother? To do this?'

Yeah. It definitely did.

'I wouldn't be much of a human being if I travelled the entire country only looking after myself. Besides, we kind of have a reciprocal arrangement going. If someone's doing something special—like media or some kind of promotion—they try to include as many others as they can. This is something I can do in the big centres while taking a break from the road.'

Though Esperance was hardly a metropolis and talking to strangers all day wasn't much of a break.

He stopped just in front of her, picked up one of Travis's posters. 'Who's "we"?'

'The network.'

The sunglasses tipped more towards her.

'The missing-persons network,' she explained. 'The families. There are a lot of us.'

'You have a formal network?'

'We have an informal one. We share information. Tips. Successes.'

Failures. Quite a lot of failures.

'Good to have the support, I guess.'

He had no idea. Some days her commitment to a bunch of people she'd never met face to face was the only thing that got her out of bed.

'When I first started up, I kept my focus on Trav. But these people—' she tipped her head back towards all the faces on her poster display '—are like extended family to me because they're the family of people I'm now close to. How could I not include them amongst *The Missing*?'

A woman stopped to pick up one of her fliers and Eve quickly delivered her spiel, smiling and making a lot of eye contact. Pumping it with energy. Whatever it took…

Marshall waited until the woman had finished perusing the whole display. *'The Missing?'*

She looked behind her. 'Them.'

And her brother had the biggest and most central poster on it.

He nodded to a gap on the top right of the display. 'Looks like one's fallen off.'

'I just took someone down.'

His eyebrows lifted. 'They were found? That's great.'

No, not great. But at least found. That was how it was for the families of long-timers. The Simmons family had the rest of their lives to deal with the mental torture that came with feeling *relief* when their son's remains were found in a gully at the bottom of a popular hiking mountain. Closure. That became the goal somewhere around the ten-month mark.

Emotional euthanasia.

Maybe one day that would be her—loathing herself for being grateful that the question mark that stalked her twenty-four-seven was now gone because her brother was. But there was no way she could explain any of that to someone outside the network. Regular people just didn't get it. It was just so much easier to smile and nod.

'Yes. Great.'

Silence clunked somewhat awkwardly on the table between them.

'Did you get out to Israelite Bay yet?' he finally asked.

'I'll probably do that tomorrow or Wednesday.'

His clear eyes narrowed. 'Listen. I have an idea. You need to travel out to the bay and I need to head out to Cape Arid and Middle Island to survey them for a possible new weather station. Why don't we team up, head out together? Two birds, one stone.'

More together time in which to struggle with conversation and obsess about his tattoos. Was that wise?

'I'll only slow you down. I need to do poster drops at all roadhouses, caravan parks and campsites between here and there.'

'That's okay. As far as the office is concerned, I have a couple of days while the truck mess is cleared up. We can take our time.'

Why did he seem so very reluctant? Almost as if

he was speaking against his will. She scrunched her nose as a prelude to an *I don't think so.*

But he beat her to it. 'Middle Island is off-limits to the public. You can't go there without a permit.'

'And you have a permit?'

'I do.'

'Have you forgotten that this isn't a tourist trip for me?'

'You'll get your work done on the way, and then you'll just keep me company for mine.'

'I can get my work done by myself and be back in Esperance by nightfall.'

'Or you can give yourself a few hours off and see a bit of this country that you're totally missing.'

'And why should I be excited by Middle Island?'

'A restricted island could be a great place for someone to hide out if they don't want to be discovered.'

The moment the words left his mouth, colour peaked high on his jaw.

'Sorry—' he winced as she sucked in a breath '—that was… God, I'm sorry. I just thought you might enjoy a bit of downtime. That it might be good for you.'

But his words had had their effect. If you needed a permit and Marshall had one, then she'd be crazy not to tag along. What if she let her natural reticence stop her and Trav was there, camping and lying low?

'I'll let you ride on my bike,' he said, as though that made it better. As if it was some kind of prize.

Instantly her gut curled into a fist. 'Motorbikes kill people.'

'People kill people,' he dismissed. 'Have you ever ridden on one?'

If riding tandem with a woman in the midst of a mid-life crisis counted. 'My mother had a 250cc.'

'Really? Cool.'

Yeah, that was what she and Travis had thought, right up until the day it killed their mother and nearly him.

'But you haven't really *ridden* until you've been on a 1200.'

'No, thanks.'

'Come on… Wouldn't you like to know what it's like to have all that power between your legs?'

'If this is a line, it's spectacularly cheesy.'

He ignored that. 'Or the freedom of tearing along at one hundred clicks with nothing between you and the road?'

'You call that freedom, I call that terror.'

'How will you know until you try it?'

'I'm not interested in trying it.'

He totally failed at masking his disappointment.

'Then you can tail me in the bus. We'll convoy. It'll still be fun.'

Famous last words. Something told her the fun would run out, for him, round about the time she pulled into her third rest stop for the day, to pin up posters.

'There's also a good caravan park out there, according to the travel guides. You can watch a west coast sunset.'

'I've seen plenty of sunsets.'

'Not with me,' he said on a sexy grin.

Something about his intensity really wiggled down under her skin. Tantalising and zingy. 'Why are you so eager for me to do this?'

Grey eyes grew earnest. 'Because you're missing everything. The entire country. The moments of joy that give life its colour.'

'You should really moonlight in greeting-card messages.'

'Come on, Eve. You have to go there, anyway, it's just a few hours of detour.'

'And what if Trav comes through in those few hours?' It sounded ridiculous but it was the fear she lived with every moment of every day.

'Then he'll see one of dozens of posters and know you're looking for him.'

The simple truth of that ached. Every decision

she made ached. Each one could bring her closer to her brother or push her further away. It made decision-making pure agony. But this one came with a whole bundle of extra considerations. Marshall-shaped considerations. And the thought of sitting and watching a sunset with him even managed to alleviate some of that ache.

A surprising amount.

She sighed. 'What time?'

'How long are you set up here for?'

'I have permission to be on the waterfront until noon.'

'Five past noon, then?'

So eager. Did he truly think she was that parched for some life experience? It galled her to give him all the points. 'Ten past.'

His smile transformed his face, the way it always did.

'Done.'

'And we're sleeping separately. You know…just for the record.'

'Hey, I'm just buying you a sunset, lady.' His shrug was adorable. And totally disarming.

'Now go, Weatherman—you're scaring off my leads with all that leather.'

Her lips said 'go' but her heart said *stay*. Whispered it, really. But she'd become proficient in drowning out the fancies of her heart. And its fears. Neither were particularly productive in keeping her on track in finding Travis. A nice neutral…nothing…was the best way to proceed.

Emotionally blank, psychologically focused.

Which wasn't to say that Marshall Sullivan couldn't be a useful distraction from all the voices in her head and heart.

And a pleasant one.

And a short one.

They drove the two hundred kilometres east in a weird kind of convoy. Eve chugging along in her ancient bus and him, unable to stand the slow pace, roaring off ahead and pulling over at the turn-off to every conceivable human touch point until she caught up, whacked up a poster and headed out again. Rest stops, roadhouses, campgrounds, lookouts. Whizzing by at one hundred kilometres an hour and only stopping longer for places that had people and rubbish bins and queued-up vehicles.

It was a horrible way to see such a beautiful country.

Eventually, they made it to the campground nestled in the shoulder crook of a pristine bay on the far side of Cape Arid National Park, its land arms reaching left and right in a big, hug-like semicircle.

A haven for travellers, fishermen and a whole lot of wildlife.

But not today. Today they had the whole place to themselves.

'So many blues...' Eve commented, stepping down out of the bus and staring at the expansive bay.

And she wasn't wrong. Closer to shore, the water was the pale, almost ice-blue of gentle surf. Then the kind of blue you saw on postcards, until, out near the horizon it graduated to a deep, gorgeous blue before slamming into the endless rich blue of the Australian sky. And, down to their left, a cluster of weathered boulders were freckled by a bunch of sea lions sunning themselves.

God...so good for the soul.

'This is nothing,' he said. Compared to what she'd missed all along the south coast of Australia. Compared to what she'd driven straight past. 'If you'd just chuck your indicator on from time to time...'

She glanced at him but didn't say anything, busying stringing out her solar blanket to catch the afternoon light. When she opened the back doors of the bus to fill it with fresh sea air, she paused, looking further out to sea. Out to an island.

'Is that where we're going?'

Marshall hauled himself up next to her to follow her gaze. 'Nope. That's one of the closer, smaller islands in the archipelago. Middle Island is further out. One of those big shadows looming on the horizon.'

He leaned half across her to point further out and she followed the line of his arm and finger. It brought them as close together as they'd been since he'd dragged her kicking and cursing away from the thugs back in Norseman. And then he knew how much he'd missed her scent.

It eddied around his nostrils now, in defiance of the strong breeze.

Taunting him.

'How many are there?'

What were they talking about? Right…islands. 'More than a hundred.'

Eve stood, staring, her gaze flicking over every feature in view. Marshall kept his hand hooked around the bus's ceiling, keeping her company up there. Keeping close.

'Trav could be on any of them.'

Not if he also wanted to eat. Or drink. Only two had fresh water.

'Listen, Eve…'

She turned her eyes back up to his and it put their faces much closer than either of them might have intended.

'I really am truly sorry I said that about your

brother. It was a cheap shot.' And one that he still didn't fully understand making. He wasn't Eve's keeper. 'The chances of him being out there are—'

'Tiny. I know. But it's in my head now and I'm not going to be able to sleep if I don't chase every possibility.'

'Still, I don't want to cause you pain.'

'That's not hurting, Marshall. That's helping. It's what I'm out here for.'

She said the words extra firmly, as if she was reminding both of them. Didn't make the slightest difference to the tingling in his toes. The tingling said she was here for him.

What did toes ever know?

He held her gaze much longer than was probably polite, their dark depths giving the ocean around them a run for its money.

'Doesn't seem a particularly convenient place to put a weather station,' she said finally, turning back out to the islands.

Subtle subject change. *Not.* But he played along. 'We want remote. To give us better data on southern coastal weather conditions.'

She glanced around them at the whole lot of nothing as far as the eye could see. 'You got it.'

Silent sound cushioned them in layers. The occasional bird cry, far away. The whump of the distant waves hitting the granite face of the south coast. The thrum of the coastal breeze around them. The awkward clearing of her throat as it finally dawned on her that she was shacked up miles from anywhere—and anyone—with a man she barely knew.

'What time are we meeting the boat? And where?'

'First thing in the morning. They'll pull into the bay, then ferry us around. Any closer to Middle Island and we couldn't get in without an off-road vehicle.'

'Right.'

Gravity helped his boots find the dirt and he looked back up at Eve, giving her the space she seemed to need. 'I'm going to go hit the water before the sun gets too low.'

Her eyes said that a swim was exactly what she wanted. But the tightness in her lips said that she wasn't about to go wandering through the sand dunes somewhere this remote with a virtual stranger. Fair enough, they'd only known each other hours. Despite having a couple of life-threatening moments between them. Maybe if she saw him walking away from her, unoffended and unconcerned, she'd feel more comfortable around him. Maybe if he offered no pressure for the two of them to spend time together, she'd relax a bit.

And maybe if he grew a pair he wouldn't care.

'See you later on, then.'

Marshall jogged down to the beach without looking back. When he hit the shore he laid his boots, jeans and T-shirt out on the nearest rock to get nice and toasty for his return and waded into the ice-cold water in his shorts. Normally he'd have gone without, public or not, but that wasn't going to win him any points in the *Is it safe to be here with you?* stakes. The sand beneath his feet had been beaten so fine by the relentless Southern Ocean it was more like squidging into saturated talcum powder than abrasive granules of sand. Soft and welcoming, the kind of thing you could imagine just swallowing you up.

And you wouldn't mind a bit.

His skin instantly thrilled at the kiss of the ice-cold water after the better part of a day smothered in leather and road dust, and he waded the stretch of shallows, then dived through the handful of waves that built up momentum as the rapid rise of land forced them into graceful, white-topped arcs.

This was his first swim since Cactus Beach, a whole state away. The Great Australian Bight was rugged and amazing to look at right the way across the guts of the country but when the rocks down to the sea were fifty metres high and the ocean down there bottomless and deadly, swimming had to take a short sabbatical. But swimming was also one of the things that kept him sane and being barred from it got him all twitchy.

Which made it pretty notable that the first thing he *didn't do* when he pulled up to the beautiful, tranquil and swimmable shores of Esperance earlier today was hit the water.

He went hunting for a dark-haired little obsessive instead.

Oh, he told himself a dozen lies to justify it—that he'd rather swim the private beaches of the capes; that he'd rather swim at sunset; that he'd rather get the Middle Island review out of the way first so he could take a few days to relax—but that was all starting to feel like complete rubbish. Apparently, he was parched for something more than just salt water.

Company.

Pfff. Right. That was one word for it.

It had been months since he'd been interested enough in a woman to do something about it, and by 'interested' he meant hungry. Hungry enough to head out and find a woman willing to sleep with a man who had nothing to offer but a hard, one-off lay before blowing town the next day. There seemed to be no shortage of women across the country who were out to salve a broken heart, or pay back a cheating spouse, or numb something broken deep inside them. They were the ones he looked for when he got needy enough because they didn't ask questions and they didn't have expectations.

It took one to know one.

Those encounters scratched the itch when it grew too demanding…and they reminded him how empty and soulless relationships were. All relationships, not just the random strangers in truck stops and bars across the country. Women. Mothers.

Brothers.

At least the women in the bars knew where they stood. No one was getting used. And there was no one to disappoint except himself.

He powered his body harder, arm over arm, and concentrated on how his muscles felt, cutting his limbs through the surf. Burning from within, icy from without. The familiar, heavy ache of lactic acid building up. And when he'd done all the examination it was possible to do on his muscles, he focused on the water: how the last land it had touched was Antarctica, how it was life support for whales and elephant seals and dugongs and colossal squid and mysterious deep-trench blobs eight kilometres below the surface and thousands of odd-shaped sea creatures in between. How humans were a bunch of nimble-fingered, big-brained primates that really only used the millimetre around the edge of the mapped oceans and had absolutely no idea how much of their planet they knew nothing about.

Instant Gulliver.

It reminded him how insignificant he was in the scheme of things. Him and all his human, social problems.

The sun was low on the horizon when he next paid attention, and the south coast of Australia was littered with sharks who liked to feed at dusk and dawn. And while there had certainly been a day he would have happily taken the risk and forgotten the consequences, he'd managed to find a happy place in the *Groundhog Day* blur that was the past six months on the road, and could honestly say— hand on heart—that he'd rather not be shark food now.

He did a final lazy lap parallel with the wide beach back towards his discarded clothes, then stood as soon as the sea floor rose to meet him. His hands squeezed up over his lowered lids and back through his hair, wringing the salt water out of it, then he stood, eyes closed, with his face tipped towards the warmth of the afternoon sun.

Eventually, he opened them and started, just a little, at Eve standing there, her arms full of towel, her mouth hanging open as if he'd interrupted her mid-sentence.

* * *

Eve knew she was gaping horribly but she was no more able to close her trap than rip her eyes from Marshall's chest and belly.

His *tattooed* chest and belly.

Air sucked into her lungs in choppy little gasps.

He had some kind of massive bird of prey, wings spread and aloft, across his chest. The lower curve of its majestic wings sat neatly along the ridge of his pectorals and its wing tips followed the line of muscle there up onto his tanned, rounded shoulders. Big enough to accentuate the musculature of his chest, low enough to be invisible when he was wearing a T-shirt. It should have been trashy but it wasn't; it looked like he'd been born with it.

His arms were still up, squeezing the sea water from his hair, and that gave her a glimpse of a bunch of inked characters—Japanese, maybe Chinese?—on the underside of one full biceps.

Add that to the dagger on the other arm and he had a lot of ink for a weatherman.

'Hey.'

His voice startled her gaze back to his and her tongue into action.

'Wow,' she croaked, then realised that wasn't the most dignified of beginnings. 'You were gone so long...'

Great. Not even capable of a complete sentence.

'I've been missing the ocean. Sorry if I worried you.'

She grasped around in the memories she'd just spent a couple of hours accumulating, studying the map to make sure they hadn't missed a caravan park or town. And she improvised some slightly more intelligent conversation.

'Whoever first explored this area really didn't have the best time doing it.'

Marshall dripped. And frowned. As he lowered his arms to take the towel from her nerveless fingers, the bird of prey's feathers shifted with him, just enough to catch her eye. She struggled to look somewhere other than at him, but it wasn't easy when he filled her field of view so thoroughly. She wanted to step back but then didn't want to give him the satisfaction of knowing she was affected.

'Cape Arid, Mount Ragged, Poison Creek…' she listed with an encouraging lack of wobble in her voice, her clarity restored the moment he pressed the towel to his face and disguised most of that unexpectedly firm and decorated torso.

He stepped over to the rock and hooked up his T-shirt, then swept it on in a smooth, manly shrug. Even with its overstretched neckline, the bird of prey was entirely hidden. The idea of him hanging out in his meteorological workplace in a government-appropriate suit with all of that ink hidden away under it was as secretly pleasing as when she used to wear her best lingerie to section meetings.

Back when stupid things like that had mattered.

'I guess it's not so bad when you have supplies and transport,' he said, totally oblivious to her illicit train of thought, 'but it must have been a pretty treacherous environment for early explorers. Especially if they were thirsty.'

She just blinked at him. What was he saying? What had she asked?

He didn't bother with the rest of his clothes; he just slung the jeans over his shoulder and followed her back up to camp with his boots swinging in his left hand.

'Nice swim?' Yeah. Much easier to think with all that skin and ink covered up.

'I've missed it. The water's so clean down here.'

'Isn't ocean always clean?'

'Not at all. It's so easy to imagine the Southern Ocean being melt straight from Antarctica. Beautiful.'

'Maybe I'll take a dip tomorrow.' When Marshall was otherwise engaged.

They fell to silence as they approached the bus. Suddenly the awkwardness of the situation amplified. One bus. Two people. One of them half-naked and the other fresh from a bout of uncontrollable ogling. As though her-on-the-bed and him-on-the-sofa was the only social nicety to be observed. There was a bathroom and TV space and…air to consider. She was used to having the bus entirely to herself, now she had to share it with a man for twenty-four hours. And not just any man.

A hot man.

A really hot man.

'Um. You take the bus to change, I'll just—' she looked around for inspiration and saw the quirky little public out-house in the distance '—check out the facilities.'

Oh, good Lord…

'Thanks. I'll only be a few minutes.'

Her, too. Most definitely. There was a reason she'd held out until she found a live-in transport with a toilet built into it. Public toilets in remote Australia were not for the faint of heart.

As it turned out, this one was a cut above average. Well maintained and stocked. Some kind of eco-composting number. It was only when she caught herself checking out how the pipework operated that she knew just how badly she was stalling. As if toilets were anywhere near that fascinating.

Come on, Read, man up.

Returning revealed Marshall to have been as good as his word. He was changed, loosely groomed and waiting outside the bus already. *Outside*. Almost as though he was trying to minimise his impact on her space.

He held his new bike helmet out to her.

'Come on.' He smiled. 'I promised you a ride. While we still have light.'

It took approximately twenty-five seconds for Eve to get over her concern that Marshall only had one motorbike helmet and he was holding it out to her. After that, she was all about survival of the fittest.

'I don't remember agreeing to this—'

'You'll love it, Eve. I promise.'

She glared up at him. 'Just because you do?'

'Because it's brilliant. And fun.'

No. Not always fun. She'd lost one and nearly two people she loved to a not-so-fun motorbike. Though that could just as easily have been a car, her logical side whispered. Or a bus. Or a 747. Tragedies happened every single day.

Just that day it happened to them.

'Think of it like a theme park ride,' he cajoled. 'A roller coaster.'

'That's not really helping.'

'Come on, Eve. What else are we going to do until it's dark?'

Apart from sit in the bus in awkward silence obsessing on who was going to sleep where...? She glanced sideways at the big orange bike.

'I'll keep you safe, I promise. We'll only go as fast as you're comfortable with.'

His siren voice chipped away at her resistance. And his vow—*I'll keep you safe.* For so long she'd been all about looking after her father and brother. When was the last time someone offered to look after *her*?

'Just slow?'

Of course there was small print, but it came delightfully packaged in a grin full of promise. 'Until you're ready for more.'

He seemed so incredibly confident that was going to happen. Her bottom lip wiggled its way between her teeth. She *had* always wondered what it would be like to ride something with a bit more power. If by *always* she meant after two hours of watching a leather-clad Marshall dominate the machine under him. And if by *ride* she meant pressing her thighs into his and her front to that broad, strong back, both of them hepped up on adrenaline. It was a seductive picture. The kind of picture that was best reserved for her and a quiet, deluded night in the bus.

She hadn't imagined it would ever go from fantasy to opportunity.

He held the helmet out again.

'You'll slow the moment I ask?' she breathed.

'Cross my heart.'

Yeah, not really selling it. Everyone knew what came after that line…

But it was only when she was about to lower her hand away from the helmet that she realised she'd even raised it. What was she going to do, live in fear of motorbikes for the rest of her life? No one was even sure what had caused her mother's accident—even Trav, after he'd come out of the coma, couldn't shed much light. Tragic accident. Could have happened to anyone. That was the final verdict.

'You'll drive safely?'

Come on, Read, suck it up.

Sincerity blazed in his solemn grey gaze. 'I'll be a model of conservatism.'

How long had it been since she'd done something outside of the box? Or taken any kind of risk? She used to be edgy, back before life got so very serious and she took responsibility for Travis. And her risks had almost always paid off. That was part of the thrill.

Hadn't she once been known for that?

Here was a gorgeous man offering to wrap her

around him for a little bit. And the price—a bit of reckless speed.

It had been years since she'd done something reckless. Maybe it would be good for her.

She took a deep breath and curled her fingers around the helmet's chin strap.

The KTM hit a breath-stealing speed in about the same time it took her to brave opening her eyes. The road whizzed below them in such a blur it was like riding on liquid mercury.

At least that was how it felt.

She immediately remembered the excitement of riding behind her mother, but her mother's bike had never purred like this one. And it had never glued itself to the road like the tyres on this one.

Maybe if it had, all their lives would have been very different now.

She pressed herself more fully into Marshall's hard back and practically punched her fingertips through his leather jacket from clenching it so hard.

'Is this top speed?' she yelled forward to him.

His hair whipped around above her face as he shook his head and shouted back. 'We're only doing seventy kilometres.'

'Don't go any faster,' she called.

She hated the vulnerable note in her voice, but

she hated more the thought of hitting the dirt at this kind of speed. In Travis's case it had been trees but she felt fairly certain that you didn't need trees to be pretty badly injured on a bike.

Marshall turned his face half back to her and smiled beneath his protective sunglasses, nodding once. She'd just have to trust those teeth.

The roads of the national park were long and straight and the bike sat atop them beautifully so, after a few tense minutes, Eve let her death grip on his jacket ease slightly and crept them back to rest on Marshall's hips instead. Still firm, but the blood was able to leach back into her knuckles.

For a death machine he handled it pretty well.

Ahead, the road bent around a monolithic chunk of rock and he eased off the gas to pass it carefully. The bike's lean felt extreme to her and her grasp on his leather jacket completely insufficient, so her fingers found their way under it and hooked onto the eyelets of his jeans.

A few paltry sweatshop stitches were the only thing between her and certain doom.

While the engine was eased, Marshall took the opportunity to call back to her, half turning, 'Doing okay?'

Eyes front, mister!

'Stop staring down,' he shouted. 'Look around you.'

She let her eyes flutter upwards as he turned his attention back to the oncoming road. The entire park was bathed in the golden glow of afternoon light, the many different textures changing the way the light reflected and creating the golden equivalent of the ocean. So many different shades.

And—bonus—the speed didn't seem anywhere near as scary as staring down at the asphalt.

It was almost like being in the Bedford. Sans life-saving steel exoskeleton.

She didn't want to look like a complete wuss, and so Eve did her best to ease herself back from where her body had practically fused with his. The problem with that was as soon as he changed up gears, she brushed, breasts first, against his back. And then again.

And again, as he shifted up into fourth.

Okay, now he was just messing with her. She was having a difficult enough reaction to all that leather without adding to the crisis by torturing her own flesh. Leaning into him might be more intimate, but it felt far less gratuitous and so she snuggled forward again, widening her legs to fit more snugly around his. Probably not how a passenger was supposed to ride—the fact her bottom had left the pillion seat in favour of sharing his leathery saddle proved that—

but that was how it was going to be for her first ever big boy's motorcycle experience.

And if he didn't like it he could pull over.

Minutes whizzed by and she grew captivated by the long stretches of tufted grass to her left, the parched, salt-crusted trees and coastal heath to her right and the limestone outcrops that practically glowed in the late-afternoon light. So much so that, when Marshall finally pulled them to a halt at a lookout point, she realised she'd forgotten all about the speed. Her pulse was up, her exposed skin was flushed pink and her breath was pleasantly choppy.

But she hadn't died.

And she wasn't ready for it to be over.

'I can see why she—why *you* like this,' she puffed, lifting the visor on her helmet and leaning around him. 'It's a great way to see the country.'

'Are you comfortable?'

His innocuous words immediately reminded her of how close she was pressed against him—wrapped around him, really—and she immediately went to correct that.

'Stay put,' he cautioned. 'We're about to head back.'

She leaned with him as he turned the bike in a big arc on an old salt flat and then bumped back onto the tarmac. As if she'd been doing this forever. And, as he roared back up to speed, she realised how very much in the *now* she'd been. Just her, Marshall, the road, the wind and the national park.

No past. No future. No accidents. No inquests. No Travis.

And how nice that moment of psychological respite was.

The light was totally different heading back. Less golden. More orange. And fading fast. He accessed a fifth gear that he'd spared her on the first leg and even still, when he pulled back in near the bus, the sun was almost gone. She straightened cold-stiffened limbs and pulled off his helmet.

'How was that?' he asked, way more interest in his eyes than a courtesy question. He kicked the stand into position and leaned the bike into the solid embrace of the earth.

'Amazing.'

The word formed a tiny breath cloud in the cool evening air and it was only then she realised how cold she was. The sun's warmth sure departed fast in this part of the country.

He followed her back towards the bus. 'You took a bit to loosen up.'

'Considering how terrified I was, I don't think I did too badly.'

'Not badly at all. I felt the moment when the fear left your body.'

The thought that she'd been pressed closely enough to him to be telegraphing any kind of emotion caused a rush of heat that she was very glad it was too dim for him to see. But he stepped ahead of her and opened the back of the Bedford and caught the last vestiges of her flush.

'How are you feeling now about motorcycles?'

His body blocked the step up into the bus and so she had no choice but to brush past him as she pulled herself up.

'It's still a death trap,' she said, looking back down at him. 'But not entirely without redeeming qualities.'

Not unlike its owner, really.

CHAPTER FOUR

'I WAS THINKING of steak and salad for dinner,' Eve said, returning from her little bedroom newly clad in a sweater to take the edge off the cool coastal night.

Lord, how domestic. And utterly foreign.

'You don't need to cook for me, Eve. I ate up big at lunchtime in anticipation.'

'I was there, remember? And while it certainly was big you probably burned it all off with that epic swim earlier.'

And Lord knew, between the lusting and the fearing for her life, she'd just burnt all hers off, too.

Preparing food felt natural; she'd been doing it for Travis for so many years. Moreover, it gave her something constructive and normal to do for thirty minutes, but Marshall wasn't so lucky. He hovered, hopelessly. After the comparative intimacy of the bike ride, it seemed ludicrous to be uncomfortable about sharing a simple meal. But he was, a little.

And so was she. A lot.

'Here.' She slid him a bottle opener across the

raw timber counter of the Bedford's compact little kitchen. 'Make yourself useful.'

She nodded to a small cabinet above the built-in television and, when he opened it, his eyebrows lifted at the contents. 'I thought you didn't drink?'

That rattled a chuckle from her tight chest.

'Not in bars—' with men she didn't know, and given her familial history '—but I like to sample the local wines as I move around.'

She brought her solitary wineglass out from under the bench, then added a coffee mug next to it. The best she could do.

'You take the glass,' she offered.

He took both, in fact, poured two generous servings of red and slid the wineglass back her way. 'I guess you don't entertain much?'

'Not really out here for the social life,' she said. But then she relented. 'I did have a second glass once but I have no idea where it's gone. So it's the coffee mug or it's my toothbrush glass.'

And didn't that sound pathetic.

'You're going to need another storage cupboard,' he murmured, bringing the mug back from his lips and licking the final drops off, much to her sudden fascination. 'We're headed for serious wine country.'

'Maybe I just need to drink faster.'

He chuckled and saluted her with the mug. 'Amen to that.'

What was it about a communal glass of vino that instantly broke down the awkwardness barrier? He'd only had one sip and she'd had none, yet, so it wasn't the effects of the alcohol. Just something about popping a cork and swilling a good red around in your glass—or coffee mug—the great equaliser.

Maybe that was how her mother had begun. Social and pleasant. Until one day she woke up and it wasn't social any more. Or pleasant.

'So tell me,' Eve started, continuing with her food prep, 'did you have much competition for half a year in the bush checking on weather stations?'

He smiled and leaned across to relieve her of the chopping knife and vegetables from the fridge. 'I did not.'

It was too easy to respond to that gentle smile. To let her curiosity have wings. To tease. 'Can't imagine why not. Why did you accept it?'

'Travel the country, fully paid. What's not to love?'

'Being away from your friends and family?'

Being away from your girlfriend. She concentrated hard to keep her eyes from dropping to the bottom of the biceps dagger that peeked out from under his sleeve.

'Not all families benefit from being in each other's faces,' he said, a little tightly.

She stopped and regarded him. 'Speaking from experience?'

Grey eyes flicked to hers.

'Maybe. Don't tell me,' he nudged. 'You have the perfect parents.'

Oh...so far from the truth it was almost laughable. The steaks chuckled for her as she flipped them. 'Parent singular. Dad.'

He regarded her closely. 'You lost your mum?'

'Final year of school.'

'I'm sorry. New subject?'

'No. It's a long time ago now. It's okay.'

'Want to talk about it?'

Sometimes, desperately. Sometimes when she sat all alone in this little bus that felt so big she just wished she had someone sitting there with her that she could spill it all to. Someone to help her make sense of everything that had happened. Because she still barely understood it.

'Not much to talk about. She was in an accident. Travis was lucky to survive it.'

His fathomless gaze grew deeper. Full of sympathy. 'Car crash?'

Here it came...

'Motorbike, actually.'

His eyes flared and he spun more fully towards her. 'Why didn't you say, Eve?'

'I'm saying now.'

'Before I press-ganged you into taking a ride with me,' he gritted, leaning over the counter.

'I could have said no. At any time. I'm not made of jelly.' Except when Marshall smiled at her a certain way. Then anyone would be forgiven for thinking so.

'I never would have—'

'It wasn't the bike's fault. It's good for me to remember that.'

He took a long, slow breath and Eve distracted herself poking the steaks.

'A 250cc, you said. Not your usual family wagon.'

'Oh, we had one of those, too. But she got her motorcycle licence not long after having Travis.' Like some kind of statement. 'She rode it whenever she didn't have us with her.'

Which was often in those last five years.

'I think it was her way of fighting suburbia,' she murmured.

Or reality, maybe.

'But she had your brother with her that day?' Then, 'Are you okay to talk about this?'

Surprisingly, she was. Maybe because Marshall was a fellow motorbike fanatic. It somehow felt okay for him to know.

'Yeah—' she sighed '—she did. Trav loved her bike. He couldn't wait to get his bike permit. I think she was going to give him the Kawasaki. He'd started to learn.'

'How old was he when it happened?'

'Fourteen.'

'Five years between you. That's a biggish gap.'

'Thank God for it. Not sure I could have handled any of it if I'd been younger.'

It was hard enough as it was.

It was only when Marshall's voice murmured, soft and low, over her shoulder and he reached past her to turn off the gas to the steaks that she realised how long she'd been standing there mute. Her skin tingled at his closeness.

'New subject?'

'No. I'm happy to talk about my family. I just forget sometimes…'

'Forget what?'

Sorrow washed through her. 'That my family's different now. That it's just me and Dad.'

'You say that like…'

Her eyes lifted. 'That's the reality. If Trav is missing by force, then he's not coming back. And if he's missing by choice…'

Then he's not coming back.

Either way, her already truncated family had shrunk by one more.

'You really believe he could be out here somewhere, just…lying low?'

'I have to believe that. That he's hurting. Confused. Off his meds. Maybe he doesn't think he'd be welcome back after leaving like he did. I want him to know we want him back no matter what.'

Marshall's head bobbed slowly. 'No case to answer? For the distress he's caused?'

Her hand fell still on the spatula. For the longest time, the only sound came from the low-burn frying pan. But, eventually, her thoughts collected into something coherent.

'I ask myself is there anything he could do that would make me not want to have him back with us and the answer is no. So giving him grief for what he did, or why he did it, or the manner in which he did it… It has no purpose. I just want him to walk back in that door and scuff the wall with his school bag and start demanding food. The *what*, *why* and *how* is just not relevant.'

Intelligent eyes glanced from her still fingers to her face. 'It's relevant to you.'

'But it's not important. In the scheme of things.'

Besides, she already had a fairly good idea of the *why*. Travis's escalating anxiety and depression seemed blazingly obvious in hindsight, even if she hadn't seen it at the time. Because she hadn't been paying attention. She'd been far too busy shrugging off her substitute mother apron.

Thinking about herself.

She poked at the steak again and delicious juices ran from it and added to the noise in the pan. She lifted her wineglass with her free hand and emptied a bit into the pan. Then she took a generous swig and changed the subject.

'So, who is Christine?'

No-man's-land the last time they spoke, but they weren't spending the night under the same roof then. They barely knew each other then.

We barely know each other now! a tiny voice reminded her.

But they did. Maybe not a heap of details, but they knew each other's names and interests and purpose. She'd seen him half naked striding out of the surf, and she'd pressed up against him a grand total of two times now and had a different kind of glimpse at the kind of man he was under all the leather and facial hair. He struck her as...safe.

And sometimes safe was enough.

But right now *safe* didn't look entirely happy at her words. Though he still answered.

'Was,' he clarified. 'Christine was my girlfriend.'

Clang. The pan hit the stovetop at his use of the past tense. There was the answer to a question she didn't know she'd been dying to ask. Unexpected butterflies took flight deep in her gut and she busied herself with a second go at moving the frying pan off the heat.

'Recent?'

His strong lips pursed briefly as he considered answering. Or not answering. 'Long time ago.'

Yeah, the ink didn't look new, come to think of it. Unlike the one she'd seen under his biceps.

Which meant he could still be someone else's hairy biker type. That she was having a quiet steak with. Under a gem-filled sky. Miles from anywhere. After a blood-thrilling and skin-tingling motorbike ride...

She shook the thoughts free. 'Childhood sweetheart?'

Tension pumped off him. 'Something like that.'

And suddenly she disliked Christine intensely. 'I'm sorry.'

He shrugged. 'Not your doing.'

She studied the tight lines at the corner of his mouth. The mouth she'd not been able to stop looking at since he'd shaved and revealed it. Tonight was no different. 'So...there's no Christine now? I mean someone like Christine?'

His eyes found hers. 'You asking if I'm single?'

'Just making conversation. I figured not, since you were on a pilgrimage around the country.'

'It's my job, Eve. Not everyone out here is on some kind of odyssey.'

That stung as much as the sea salt she'd accidentally rubbed in her eye earlier. Because of the judgment those words contained. And the truth. And because they came from him.

But he looked contrite the moment they fell off his lips.

'You don't like talking about her, I take it?' she murmured.

He shook his head but it was no denial.

'Fair enough.' Then she nodded at his arm. 'You might want to get that altered though.'

The tension left his face and a couple of tiny smile lines peeked out the corners of his eyes. 'I couldn't have picked someone with a shorter name, huh? Like Ann. Or Lucy.'

Yep. Christine sure was a long word to tattoo over.

'It's pretty florid, too. A dagger?'

The smile turned into a laugh. 'We were seventeen and in love. And I fancied myself for a bit of a tough guy. What can I say?'

Eve threw some dressing on the salad and gave it a quick toss.

'She got a matching one I hope?'

'Hers just said *Amore*. Multi-purpose.'

'*Pfff*. Non-committal. That should have been your first warning.'

She added a steak to each of their plates.

'With good reason, it turns out.'

'Christine sucked?'

That earned her a chuckle. She loved the rich, warm sound because it came from so deep in his chest. 'No, she didn't. Or I wouldn't have fallen for her.'

'That's very charitable.'

He waved his coffee mug. 'I'm a generous guy.'

'So...I'm confused,' she started. 'You don't want to talk about her, but you don't hold it against her?'

'It's not really about Christine,' he hedged.

'What isn't?' And then, when he didn't respond, 'The awkward silence?'

'How many people end up with their first love, really?'

She wouldn't know. She hadn't had time for love while she was busy raising her family. Or since. More's the pity.

'So where did she end up?'

The look he gave her was enigmatic. But also appraising. And kind of stirring. 'Not important.'

'You're very complicated, Marshall Sullivan.'

His smile crept back. 'Thank you.'

Eve leaned across the counter and lifted the hem of his sleeve with two fingers to have a good look at the design. Her fingertips brushed the smooth strength of his warm biceps and tingled where they travelled.

She cleared her throat. 'Maybe you could change it to *pristine*, like the ocean? That way, you only have to rework the first two letters.'

Three creases formed across his brow as he looked down. 'That could actually work...'

'Or *Sistine*, like the chapel.'

'Or *intestine*, like the pain I get from smelling that steak and not eating it.'

They loaded their plates up with fresh salad and both tucked in.

'This is really good.'

'That surprises you?'

'I didn't pick you as a cook.'

She shrugged. 'I had a rapid apprenticeship after Mum died.'

She munched her way through half her plate before speaking again.

'Can I ask you something personal?'

'Didn't you already do that?'

'About travelling.'

His head tilted. 'Go ahead.'

'Do you...' Lord, how to start this question? 'You travel alone. Do you ever feel like you've forgotten how to be with somebody else? How to behave?'

'What do you mean?'

'I just...I used to be so social. Busy schedule, urban lifestyle, dinners out most evenings. Meeting new people and chatting to them.' Up until the accident, anyway. 'I feel like I've lost some of my social skills.'

'Honestly?'

She nodded.

'Yeah, you're missing a few of the niceties. But once you get past that, you're all right. We're conversing happily now, aren't we?'

Give or take a few tense undercurrents.

'Maybe you just got good at small talk,' he went on. 'And small talk doesn't take you far in places like this. Situations like this. It's no good at all in silence. It just screams. But we're doing okay, on the whole.'

She rushed to correct him. 'I didn't mean you, specifically—'

'Yeah, you did.'

'What makes you say that?'

'Eve, this feels awkward because it *is* awkward. We don't know each other and yet I was forced into your world unnaturally. And now a virtual stranger is sitting ten feet from your bed, drinking your wine and getting personal. Of course it's uncomfortable.'

'I'm not…it's not uncomfortable, exactly. I just feel really rusty. And you don't deserve that. You've been very nice.'

The word *nice* hit him visibly. He actually winced.

'When was the last time you had someone in your bus?' he deviated.

Eve racked her brain… Months. Lots of months. 'Long enough for that second wineglass to end up right at the back of some cupboard.'

'There you go, then. You're out of shape, socially, that's all.'

She stared at him.

'Let's make a pledge. I promise to be my clunky self when you're around if you'll do the same.' He drew a big circle around the two of them and some tiny part of her quite liked being in that circle with him. 'This is a clunk-approved zone.'

'Clunk-approved?'

'Weird moments acknowledged, accepted and for-given.'

Why was it so easy to smile, with him? 'You're giving me permission to be socially clumsy?'

'I'm saying I'll understand.'

It was so much easier to breathe all of a sudden. 'All right. Sounds good.'

And on that warm and toasty kindred-spirit moment…

'Are you done?' she checked.

He scooped the last of his steak into his mouth and nodded.

'Hop up, I'd like to show you something.'

As soon as he stood up and back, she pinched the tall stool out from under him and clambered onto it. That allowed her to pop the latch on what looked to anyone else like a sunroof. It folded back onto the bus with a thump. She boosted herself up and into the void, wriggling back until her bottom was thoroughly seated and her legs dangled down into the bus.

'Pass the wine up,' she asked.

He did, but not before adding a generous splash to both their vessels. Then he hoisted himself up opposite her—disgustingly effortlessly—and followed her gaze, left, up out into the endless, dark sky over the Southern Ocean.

'Nice view.'

Essentially the same view as when they'd stood up on the Bedford's back step, just a little higher, but somehow it was made all the more spectacular by the location, the wine and the darkness.

And the company.

'I like to do this when the weather's fine.' Though usually alone.

'I can see why.'

The sky was blanketed with light from a gazillion other solar systems. The full you'll-never-see-it-in-the-city cliché. Eve tipped her head back, stared up and sighed.

'Sometimes I feel like I might as well be looking for Trav out there.' She tossed her chin to the trillions of unseen worlds orbiting those million stars. 'It feels just as unachievable.'

He brought his eyes back down from the heavens. Back to hers.

'It was such a simple plan when I set off. Visit every town in Australia and put posters up. Check for myself. But all it's done is reinforce for me how vast this country is and how many ways there are for someone to disappear. Living or dead.'

'It's a good plan, Eve. Don't doubt yourself.'

She shrugged.

'Did you do it because you truly thought you'd find him? Or did you do it because you had to do something?'

Tears suddenly sprang up and she fought them. It took a moment to get the choke out of her words.

'He's so young. Still a kid, even if the law says otherwise. I was going crazy at home. Waiting. Hoping each day would be the day that the police freed up enough time to look into Trav's case a bit. Made some progress. My heart leaping every time the phone rang in case it was news.'

Fighting endlessly with her father, who wanted her to give up. To accept the truth.

His truth.

'So here you are,' he summarised, simply. 'Doing something constructive. Does it feel better?'

'Yeah. When it's not feeling totally futile.'

It was too dark for the colour of his eyes to penetrate, but his focus fairly blazed out from the shadows under his sockets. 'It's only futile when it stops achieving anything. Right now it's keeping you sane.'

How did this total stranger know her better than anyone else—better than she knew herself?

Maybe because it took one to know one.

She saluted him with her wine. 'Well, aren't we a pack of dysfunctional sad sacks.'

'I'm not sad,' Marshall said, pretty proudly.

What was his story? Curiosity burnt, bright and blazing. The intense desire to *know* him.

'Nothing to say about being dysfunctional?'

'Nope. Totally guilty on that charge.'

The wind had changed direction the moment the sun set, and its heat no longer affected the vast pockets of air blanketing the southern hemisphere. They were tickled by its kiss but no longer buffeted, and it brought with it a deep and comfortable silence.

'So,' Marshall started, 'if I want to use the bus's bathroom during the night I'm basically in your bedroom, right? How's that going to work?'

She just about gave herself whiplash glancing up at him.

'Uh...'

The bus's little en suite bathroom was on the other side of the door that separated it from the rest of the bus. And from Marshall.

Groan. Just another practicality she hadn't thought through thoroughly.

That's because you just about fell over yourself to travel with him for a bit.

'Or I can use the campsite toilet,' he suggested.

Yes! Thank the Lord for public services.

'It's not too bad, actually.' If you didn't mind rocks on your bare feet at three in the morning and spiders in the dark. 'What time do we need to be up?'

As soon as the words tumbled over her lips she regretted them. Why was she ending the moment of connection so soon after it had begun?

'The boat's coming at eight.'

And dawn was at six. That was two hours of daylight for the two of them to enjoy sharing the clunk-approved zone together. 'Okay. I'll be ready.'

He passed her his mug, then swung himself down and in and took it and hers and placed them together on the bench below. Eve wiggled to the edge of the hatch and readied her arms to take her weight.

'You all right?'

'Yeah, I do it all the time.' Though she just half tumbled, half swung, usually. Gravity fed. Completely inelegant. 'I don't normally have an audience for this bit.'

His deep voice rumbled, 'Here, let me help...'

Suddenly two strong hands were around her waist, pressed sure and hot against her midriff, and she had no choice but to go with them through the roof and back inside the bus. Marshall eased her down in a far less dramatic manner than she was used to, but not without bunching her sweater up under her breasts and leaving her stomach totally exposed as she slid the length of his body. Fortunately, there were no bare hands on bare skin moments, but it was uncomfortable enough to feel the press of his cold jeans stud against her suddenly scorched tummy.

'Thanks,' she breathed.

He released her and stood back, his lashes lowered. 'No problem.'

Instantly, she wondered what the Japanese symbol for 'awkward' was and whether she'd find that tattooed anywhere on his body.

And instantly she was thinking about hidden parts of his body.

She shook the thought free. 'Well...I guess I'll see you in the morning. I'll try and be quiet if you're not up.'

'I'll be up,' he pledged.

Because he was an early riser or because he wasn't about to let her see him all tousled and vulnerable?

Or because all the touching and sliding was going to keep him awake all night, too.

CHAPTER FIVE

IT HAD BEEN a long time since Marshall had woken to the sounds of someone tiptoeing around a kitchen. In this particular case, it was extra soft because the kitchen was only two metres from his makeshift bed.

He'd heard Eve wake up, start moving around beyond that door that separated them all night, but then he'd fallen back into a light morning doze to the entirely feminine soundtrack. You had to live with someone to enjoy those moments. And you had to love them to live with them. And trust them to love them.

Unfortunately, trust and he were uneasy companions.

He'd been in one relationship post-Christine—a nice girl with lots of dreams—and that hadn't ended well. Him, of course. Just another reminder why going solo was easier on everyone concerned. Family included.

Thoughts of his brother robbed him of any further shut-eye. He pulled himself upright and forked fingers through his bed hair.

'Morning,' Eve murmured behind him. 'I hope I didn't wake you?'

'No. I was half awake, anyway. What time is it?'

'Just after six.'

Wow. Went to show what fresh air, hours of swimming and a good drop of red could do for a man's insomnia. He sure couldn't attribute it to the comfort of his bed. Every muscle creaked as he sat up, including the ones in his voice box.

'Not comfortable?'

'Better than my swag on the hard outback dirt.' Even though it really wasn't. There was something strangely comfortable about bedding down on the earth. It was very…honest. 'I'll be back in a tick.'

The morning sun was gentle but massively bright and he stumbled most of the way towards the camp-site toilet. Even with her not in her room, the thought of wedging all of himself into that compact little en suite bathroom… It was just too personal.

And he didn't do personal.

'I have eggs or I have sausages,' she announced when he walked back in a little later. 'They won't keep much longer so I'm cooking them all up.'

'Nah. I'll be all right.'

'You have to eat something; we're going to be on the water all day.'

'That's exactly why I don't want something.'

She stopped and stared. 'Do you get seasick?'

'Doesn't really fit with the he-man image you have of me, does it?' He slid back onto his stool from the night before and she passed him a coffee. 'Not horribly. But bad enough.'

'How about some toast and jam, then?'

She was determined to play host. 'Yeah, that I could do.'

That wouldn't be too disgusting coming back up in front of an audience.

She added two pieces of frozen bread to the toaster and kept on with her fry-up. If nothing else, the seagulls would love the sausages.

'Is that okay?' she said when she finally slid the buttered toast towards him.

'Just trying to think when was the last time I had toast and jam.' Toast had been about all his mother stretched to when he was a kid. But there was seldom jam.

'Not a breakfast person?'

'In the city I'd grab something from a fast food place near work.'

'I'm sure your blood vessels were grateful.'

Yeah... Not.

'Mostly it was just coffee.' The liquid breakfast of champions.

'What about out here?'

'Depends. Some motels throw a cooked breakfast in with the room. That's not always a nice surprise.'

'Well, this is a full service b & b, so eat up.'

Eating with a woman at six o'clock in the morning should have felt wrong but it didn't. In fact, clunk-approved zone moments aside, he felt pretty relaxed around Eve most of the time. Maybe because she was uptight enough for the both of them.

'Marshall?'

'Sorry. What did you say?'

'I wondered how the boat would know where to come and get us?'

'They'll just putter along the coast until they see us waving.'

'You're kidding.'

'Well, me waving, really. They're not expecting two.'

'That's very casual,' she said. 'What if they don't come?'

'Then I'll call them and they'll come tomorrow.'

Dark eyebrows shot up. 'You're assuming I'd be happy to stay an extra night.'

'If not, we could just head back to Esperance and

pick up the boat there,' he admitted. 'That's where it's moored.'

Her jaw gaped. 'Are you serious? Then why are we here?'

'Come on, Eve. Tell me you didn't enjoy the past twenty-four hours. Taking a break. Enjoying the scenery.'

Her pretty eyes narrowed. 'I feel like I've been conned.'

'You have—' he grinned around the crunch of toast smeared with strawberry jam '—by the best.'

She didn't want to laugh—her face struggled with it—but there was no mistaking the twisted smile she tried to hide by turning and plating up her eggs. Twisted and kind of gorgeous. But all she said was...

'So, talk to me about the island.'

The boat came. The *Vista II*'s two-man crew easily spotted the two of them standing on the rocks at the most obvious point of the whole beach. One of them manoeuvred a small inflatable dinghy down onto the stillest part of the early-morning beach to collect them.

The captain reached down for Eve's hands and pulled her up onto the fishing vessel and Marshall gave her a boost from below. Quite a personal boost—both of his hands starting on her waist but sliding onto her bum to do the actual shoving. Then he scrambled up without assistance and so did the old guy who had collected them in the dinghy that he hastily retethered to the boat.

'Thanks for that,' she murmured sideways to Marshall before smiling broadly at the captain and thanking him for real.

'Would you have preferred fish-scaly sea-dog hands on your butt?' Marshall murmured back.

Yeah. Maybe. Because she wouldn't have had to endure his heat still soaking into her. She already had enough of a fascination with his hands...

The next ten minutes were all business. Life vests secured, safety lecture given, seating allocated. Hers was an old square cray pot. Marshall perched on a box of safety gear.

'How long is the trip to Middle Island?' she asked the captain as soon as they were underway.

'Twenty minutes. We have to go around the long way to avoid the wrecks.'

'There are shipwrecks out here?' But as she turned and looked back along the one-hundred-strong shadowy islands of the Recherche Archipelago stretching out to the west, the question suddenly felt really foolish.

Of course there were. It was like a visible minefield of islands.

'Two right off Middle Island.'

As long as they didn't add the *Vista II* to that list, she'd be happy. 'So almost no one comes out here?'

'Not onto the islands, but there's plenty of fishing and small boating traffic.'

'And no one's living on Middle Island?'

Marshall's eyes glanced her way.

'Not since the eighteen-thirties, when Black Jack Anderson based himself and his pirating outfit there,' the captain volunteered.

Huh. So it *could* be lived on. Technically.

Eve turned her gaze towards the distant shadow that was becoming more and more defined as the boat ate up the miles and the captain chatted on about the island's resident pirate. Maybe Marshall's theory wasn't so far-fetched. Maybe Trav could be there. Or have been there in the past. Or—

And as she had the thought, she realised.

Travis.

She'd been awake two whole hours and not given her brother the slightest thought. Normally he was on her mind when her eyes fluttered open each day and the last thing she thought about at night. It kept her focused and on mission. It kept him alive in her heart.

But last night all she'd been able to think about was the man settling in just metres and a bit of flimsy timber away from her. How complicated he was. How easy he was to be around. How good he smelled.

She'd been pulled off mission by the first handsome, broad-shouldered distraction to come along. Nice. As if she wasn't already excelling at the Bad Sister of the Year award.

Well… No more.

Time to get back in the game.

'Eve?' Marshall's voice drifted to her over the sound of the outboard. 'Are you okay?'

She kept her eyes carefully averted, as though she was focusing on the approaching island, and lied.

'Just thinking about what it would be like to live there…'

They travelled in silence, but Eve could just about feel the moments when Marshall would let his eyes rest on her briefly. Assessing. Wondering. The captain chatted on with his semitour talk. About the islands. About the wildlife. About the wallabies and frogs and some special lizard that all lived in harmony on the predator-free island. About the southern rock lobster and abalone that he and his mate fished out of these perilous waters. About how many sharks there were lurking in the depths around them.

The promise of sharks made her pay extra attention as she slid back down the side of the *Vista II* into the inflatable and, before long, her feet were back on dry land. Dry, deserted land.

One glance around them at the remote, untouched, uninhabitable terrain told her Trav wasn't hiding out here.

As if there'd really been a chance.

'Watch where you step. The barking gecko is protected on this island.'

'Of course it is,' she muttered.

Marshall just glanced at her sideways. The fishermen left and promised to return for them in a couple of hours. A nervous anxiety filled her belly. If they didn't return, what would she do? How would she survive here with just a day's supply of water and snacks and no shelter? Just because Black Jack Whatsit got by for a decade didn't mean she'd last more than a day.

'So,' Marshall said after helping to push the inflatable back offshore, 'you want to explore on your own or come with me?'

Explore on my own—that was the right answer. But, at the same time, she didn't know anything about this strange little island and she was just as likely to break her ankle on the farthest corner from Marshall and his little first-aid kit.

'Is it safe?' she asked, screening her eyes with her hands and scanning the horizon.

'If you don't count the death adders, yeah.'

She snapped her focus straight back to him. 'Are you kidding?'

'Nope. But if you're watching out for the geckos you'll almost certainly see the snakes before you tread on them.'

Almost certainly.

'I'm coming with you.'

'Good choice. Feel like a climb?' She turned and followed his gaze up to the highest point on the island. 'Flinders Peak is where the weather station would go.'

He assured her it was only one hundred and eighty-five metres above sea level but it felt like Everest when you were also watching every footfall for certain death—yours or a protected gecko's.

Marshall pointed out the highlights to the west, chatted about the nearest islands and their original names. Then he halted his climb and just looked at her.

'What?' she asked, puffing.

'I'm waiting for you to turn around.'

They'd ascended the easiest face of the peak but it had obscured most of the rest of the island from their view. She turned around now.

'Oh, my gosh!'

Pink. A crazy, wrong, enormous bubblegum-pink lake lay out on the eastern corner of the island. Somehow everyone had failed to mention a bright pink lake! 'What is it?'

'Lake Hillier.'

'It's so beautiful.' But so unnatural. It just went to show how little she knew about the natural world. 'Why is it pink?'

'Bacteria? The type of salt? Maybe something new to science. Does it matter?'

'I guess not.' It was just curiously beautiful. 'Can we go there?'

'We just got up here.'

'I know, but now I want to go there.'

So much! A bit like riding on his bike, little moments of pleasure managed to cut through her miserable thoughts about Travis.

He smiled, but it was twisted with curiosity. And something else.

'What?' she queried.

'This is the first time I've seen you get really passionate about anything since I met you.'

'Some things are just worth getting your pulse up about.' And, speaking of which...

He stepped a little closer and her heartbeat responded immediately.

'Lakes and lizards do it for you?'

'*Pink* lakes and geckos that *bark*,' she stressed for

the slow of comprehension. Right on cue, a crack of vocalisation issued from a tuft of scrubby foliage to their left. She laughed in delight. But then she caught his expression.

'Seriously, Marshall… *What?*' His focus had grown way too intense. And way too pointed. She struggled against the desire to match it.

'Passion suits you. You should go hiking more often.'

Her chest had grown so tight with the climb, his words worsened her breathlessness. She pushed off again for the final peak. And for the pure distraction of physical distress.

'I get how the birds get here,' she puffed, changing the subject, 'and the crustaceans. But how did the mammals arrive here? And the lizards?'

For a moment, she thought he wasn't going to let it go but he did, gracefully.

'They didn't arrive, they endured. Back from when the whole archipelago were peaks connected to the mainland. There used to be a lot more until explorers came along and virtually wiped them out.'

Eve looked up at a circling sea eagle. 'You can't tell me that the geckos didn't get picked off by hungry birds, before.'

'Yeah, but in balance. They live in *refugia* here,

isolation from the world and its threats. Until the first cat overboard, anyway.'

Isolation from the world and its threats. She kind of liked the sound of that. Maybe that was what Trav was chasing when he walked out into the darkness a year ago. Emotional *refugia.*

She stumbled on a rock as she realised. Not a year ago…a year ago *tomorrow.* Not only had she failed to think about Travis for entire hours this morning but she'd almost forgotten tomorrow's depressing anniversary.

Her joy at their spectacular view drained away as surely as the water far below them dragged back across the shell-speckled beach where they'd come ashore.

Marshall extended his warm hand and took her suddenly cold one for the final haul up the granite top of Flinders Peak, and the entire south coast of Western Australia—complete with all hundred-plus islands—stretched out before them. The same sense of despair she'd felt when staring up at the stars the night before washed over Eve.

Australia was so incredibly vast and so incredibly empty.

So much freaking country to look in.

She stood, immobile, as he did what they'd come to do. Photographing. Measuring. Recording compass settings and GPS results. Taking copious notes and even some soil and vegetation samples. He threw a concerned glance at her a couple of times, until he finally closed up his pack again.

'Eve...'

'Are you done?'

'Come on, Eve—'

'I'm going to head down to the lake.' But there was no interest in her step, and no breathlessness in her words. Even she could hear the death in her voice.

'Stop.'

She did, and she turned.

'What just happened? What did I do?'

Truth sat like a stone in her gut. 'It wasn't you, Marshall. It was me.'

'What did *you* do?'

More what she didn't do.

'Eve?'

'I shouldn't be here.'

'We have a permit.'

'No, I mean I shouldn't be wasting time like this.'

'You're angry because you let yourself off the hook for a few hours?'

'I'm angry because I only have one thing to do out here. Prioritising Travis. And I didn't do that today.'

Or yesterday, if she was honest. She might have

pinned up a bunch of posters, but her memories of yesterday were dominated by Marshall.

'Your life can't only be about your brother, Eve. It's not healthy.'

Health. A bit late now to be paying attention to anyone's health. Her own. Her brother's. Maybe if she'd been more alert a couple of years back...

She took a deep breath. 'Are you done up here?'

A dozen expressions ranged across his face before he answered. But, when he did, his face was carefully neutral. 'We have a couple of hours before the boat gets back. Might as well have a look around with me.'

Fine. He could make her stay...

But he couldn't make her enjoy it.

It took the best part of the remaining ninety minutes on the island but Marshall managed to work the worst of the stiffness from Eve's shoulders. He did it with easy, undemanding conversation and by tapping her natural curiosity, pointing out endless points of interest and intriguing her with imaginary tales of the pirate Anderson and his hidden treasure that had never been recovered.

'Maybe his crew took it when they killed him.' She shrugged, still half-numb.

Cynical, but after the sad silence of the first half-hour he'd take it. 'Seems a reasonable enough motive to kill someone. You know, if you were a blood-thirsty pirate.'

'Or maybe there never was any treasure,' she posed. 'Maybe Anderson only managed to steal and trade enough to keep him and his crew alive, not to accrue a fortune. Maybe they weren't very good pirates!'

'You've seen the island now. Where would you bury it if it did exist?'

She glanced around. 'I wouldn't. It's too open here. Hard to dig up without being seen by the crew.' Her eyes tracked outward and he followed them to the guano-blanketed, rocky outcrop just beyond the shores of Middle Island. 'Maybe over there? Some random little cave or hollow?'

'Want to go look?'

She turned wide eyes on him. 'I'm not about to swim fully clothed across a shark-infested channel to an outcrop covered in bird poo filled with God knows what bacteria to hunt for non-existent trea-sure.'

'You have no soul, Evelyn Read,' he scoffed.

'I do have one and I'd prefer to keep it firmly teth-ered to my body, thanks very much.'

He chuckled. 'Fair enough. Come on, let's see if the lake looks as impressive up close.'

It didn't. Of course it didn't. Wasn't there something about rose-coloured glasses? But it wasn't a total disappointment. Still officially pink, even once Eve filled her empty water bottle with it.

'You're not planning on drinking that?' he warned.

'Nope.' She emptied it all back into the lake and tucked the empty bottle into her backpack for later recycling. 'Just trying to catch it out being trickily clear.'

They strolled around the lake the long way, then headed back down to the only decent beach on the island. A tiny but sandy cove formed between two outcrops of rocky reef. The place the boat had left them. Marshall immediately tugged his shoes and socks off and tied them to his own pack, which he stashed on a nearby rock, then made his way out a half-dozen metres from where Eve stood discovering that the sand was actually comprised of teeny-tiny white shells.

'Water's fine…' he hinted. 'Not deep enough for predators.'

She crossed her arms grumpily from the shore. 'What about a stingray?'

He splashed a little forward in the waves that washed in from the current surging between the islands. 'Surfing stingrays?'

'Where lakes are pink and lizards bark? Why not?'

'Come on, Eve. Kick your shoes off.'

She glared at him, but eventually she sank onto one hip and toed her opposite runner and sock off, then she did the same on the other foot. Though she took her sweet time putting both carefully in her pack and placing the lot next to his backpack on the hot sand.

'Welcome to heaven,' he murmured as she joined him in the shallows. Her groan echoed his as her hot and parched feet drank up the cold water, too. They stood there like that, together, for minutes. Their hearts slowing to synchronise with the waves washing up and into their little minibay.

Just…being.

'Okay,' Eve breathed, her face turned to the sky. 'This was a good idea.'

He waded a little further from her. 'My ideas are always good.'

She didn't even bother looking at him. 'Is that right?'

'Sure is.'

He reached down and brushed his fingers through the crystal-clear water then flicked two of them in her general direction.

She stiffened—in body and in lip—as the droplets hit her. She turned her head back his way and let her eyes creak open. 'Thanks for that.'

'You had to know that was going to happen.'

'I should have. You with a mental age of twelve and all.'

He grinned. 'One of my many charms.'

She flipped her cap off her head, bent down and filled it with fresh, clean water and then replaced the lot on her head, drenching herself in salty water.

'Well, that killed my fun,' he murmured.

But not his view. The capful of water had the added benefit of making parts of her T-shirt and cargos cling to the curves of her body even more than they already were. And that killed any chance of him cooling down unless he took more serious measures. He lowered himself onto his butt in the shallows and lay back, fully, in the drink.

Pants, shirt and all.

'You know how uncomfortable you're going to be going back?' Her silhouette laughed from high above him, sea water still trickling off her jaw and chin.

He starfished in the two feet of water. 'Small price to pay for being so very comfortable now.'

Even with her eyes mostly shaded by the peak of her cap, he could tell when her glance drifted his way. She was trying not to look—hard—but essentially failing. He experimented by pushing his torso up out of the water and leaning back casually on his hands.

'Easy to say…'

But her words didn't sound easy at all. In fact, they were as tight as her body language all of a sudden.

Well, wasn't *that* interesting.

He pushed to his feet and moved towards her, grinning. Primarily so that he could see her eyes again. Her hands came up, fast, in front of her.

'Don't you dare…'

But he didn't stop until he stood just a centimetre from her upturned hands. And he grinned. 'Don't dare do this, you mean?'

'Come on, Marshall, I don't want to get wet.'

'I'm not the one with a soggy cap dripping down my face.'

'No, you're just soaked entirely through.'

And, with those words, her eyes finally fell where she'd been trying so hard not to look. At his chest, just a finger flex away from her upturned hands.

'I'm beginning to see what Anderson might have liked about this island,' he murmured.

She huffed out a slow breath. 'You imagine he and his crew took the time to roll around in the shallows like seals?'

The thought of rolling around anything with Eve hadn't occurred to him today, but now it was all he could do to squeeze some less charged words past the evocative image. 'Flattering analogy.'

The *pfff* she shot out would have been perfectly at home on a surfacing seal. Her speech was still tinged with a tight breathlessness.

'You know you look good. That was the point of the whole submerge thing, wasn't it? To see how I'd react?'

Actually, getting cool had been the point. Once. But suddenly that original point seemed like a very long time ago. He dropped his voice with his glance. Straight to her lips. 'And how will you react, Eve?'

Her feminine little voice box lurched a few times in her exposed throat. 'I won't. Why would I give you the satisfaction?'

'Of what?'

'Of touching you—'

If she could have bitten her tongue off she would have just then, he was sure. 'Is that what you want to do? I'll step forward. All you have to do is ask.'

Step forward into those still-raised hands that were trembling ever so slightly now.

But she was a tough one. Or stubborn. Or both.

'And why would I do that?'

'Because you really want to. Because we're all alone on a deserted island with time to kill. And because we'll both be going our separate ways after Esperance.'

Though the idea seemed laughable now.

She swallowed, mutely.

He nudged the peak of her cap upwards with his knuckle to better read her expression and murmured, 'And because this might be the only chance we'll have to answer the question.'

Her eyes left his lips and fluttered up to his. 'What question?'

He stared at her. 'No. You have to ask it.'

She didn't, though he'd have bet any body part she wanted to.

'Tell you what, Eve, I'll make it easier for you. You don't have to ask me to do it, you just have to ask me *not* to do it.'

'Not do what?' she croaked.

He looked down at her trembling fingers. So very, very close. 'Not to step forward.'

Beneath the crystal-clear water, his left foot crept forward. Then his right matched it. The whole time he kept his glance down at the place that her palms almost pressed on his wet chest.

'Just one word, Eve. Just tell me to stop.'

But though her lips fell open, nothing but a soft breath came out of them.

'No?' His body sang with elation. 'All righty, then.'

And with the slightest muscle tweak at the backs of his legs, he tipped his torso the tiny distance it needed to make contact with Eve's waiting fingers.

CHAPTER SIX

DEAR LORD...

How long had it been since she'd touched someone like this? More than just a casual brushing glance? All that hard flesh Eve had seen on the beach—*felt* on the bike—pressed back against her fingers as they splayed out across his chest. Across the shadowy eagle that she knew lived there beneath the saturated cotton shirt. Across Marshall's strongly beating heart.

Across the slight rumble of the half-caught groan in his chest.

One he'd not meant to make public, she was sure. Something that told her he wanted this as much as she secretly did.

Or, as her fingers trembled, not so secretly, now.

Marshall was right. They weren't going to see each other again. And this might be the only chance she had to know what it felt like to have the heat of him pressed against her. To know him. To taste him.

All she had to do was move one finger. Any finger.

She'd never meant to enter some kind of self-imposed physical exile when she'd set off on this odyssey. It had just happened. And, before she knew it, she'd gone without touching a single person in any way at all for…

She sucked in a tiny breath. All of it. Eight months.

Puppies and kittens got touch deprivation, but did grown women? Was that what was making her so ridiculously fluttery now? Her father's goodbye hug was the last time she'd had anyone's arms around her and his arms—no matter how strong they'd once been back when she was little—had never felt as sure and rooted in earth as Marshall's had as he'd lowered her from the bus's roof last night. And that had been fairly innocuous.

What kind of damage could they do if they had something other than *help* in mind?

How good—how *bad*—might they feel? Just once. Before he rode off into the sunset and she never got an answer.

Only one way to find out.

Eve inched her thumb down under the ridge of one well-defined pectoral muscle. Nervously jerky. Half expecting to feel the softness of the ink feathers that she could see shadowed through the saturated T-shirt. But there was no softness, only the silken sleeve of white cotton that contained all that hard, hot muscle.

God, he so didn't feel like a weatherman.

Marshall's blazing gaze roasted down on the top of her wet head, but he didn't move. Didn't interrupt. He certainly didn't step back.

Eve trailed her butterfly fingers lightly up along the line of the feathers, up to his collarbone. Beyond it to the rigid definition of his larynx, which lurched out of touch and then back in again like the scandalous tease it was.

Strong fingers lifted to frame her face—to lift it—and he brought her eyes to his. They simmered, as bottomless as the ocean around them as he lowered his mouth towards hers.

'Ahoy!'

Tortured lungs sucked in painfully further as both their gazes snapped out to sea, towards the voice that carried to them on the onshore breeze. Eve stumbled back from all the touching into the buffeting arms of the surf.

'Bugger all decent catch to be had,' the gruff captain shouted as he motored the *Vista II* more fully around the rocks, somehow oblivious to the charged moment he'd just interrupted. 'So we headed back early.'

Irritation mingled with regret in Marshall's storm-grey depths but he masked it quickly and well. It really wasn't the captain's fault that the two of them had chosen the end of a long, warm afternoon to finally decide to do something about the chemistry zinging between them.

'Hold that thought,' he murmured low and earnest as he turned to salute the approaching boat.

Not hard to do while her body screamed in frustration at the interruption, but give her fifteen minutes… Give her the slightest opportunity to think through what she was doing with half her senses and…

Marshall was right to look anxious.

But, despite what she expected, by the time the *Vista II*'s inflatable dinghy transferred them and their gear safely on deck, Eve's awareness hadn't diminished at all. And that was easily fifteen minutes. During the half-hour sea journey back to the campsite beach that followed—past seals sunning themselves and beneath ospreys bobbing on the high currents and over a swarm of small stingrays that passed underneath—still the finely tuned attention her body was paying to Marshall didn't ebb in the slightest.

She forced conversation with the two-man crew, she faked interest in their paltry fishy catch, she smiled and was delightful and totally over-compensated the whole way back.

She did whatever she needed to shake free of the relentless grey eyes that tracked her every move.

After an emotional aeon, her feet were back on mainland sand and the captain lightly tossed their last backpack out of the inflatable and farewelled her before exchanging a few business-related words with Marshall. Moments later, her hand was in the air in a farewell, her smile firmly plastered on and she readied herself for the inevitable.

Marshall turned and locked eyes with her.

'Don't know about you,' he said, 'but I'm famished. Something about boats...'

Really? He was thinking about his stomach while hers was twisted up in sensual knots?

'Have we got any of those sausages from breakfast still in the fridge?'

Um...

Not that he was waiting for her answer. Marshall lugged his backpack up over his shoulder and hoisted hers into his free hand and set off towards the track winding from the beach to the campsite. Eve blinked after him. Had she fantasised the entire moment in the cove? Or was he just exceptional at separating moments?

That was then, this was now. Island rules, mainland rules?

What gave?

Warm beach sand collapsed under her tread as
she followed him up the track, her glare giving his
broody stare all the way back from Middle Island a
decent run for its money.

They polished off the leftover sausages as soon as
they got back to the bus. At least, Marshall ate most
of them while she showered and then she nibbled
restlessly on the last one while he did, trying very
hard not to think about how much naked man was
going on just feet from where she was sitting.

Soapy, wet, naked man.

Had the bus always been quite this warm?

'I think I would have been better off washing in
the ocean,' he announced when he walked back in
not long after, damp and clean and freshly clothed.
Well, freshly clothed in the least used of three pairs
of clothes he seemed to travel with. 'Lucky I didn't
drop the soap because I wouldn't have been able to
retrieve it.'

'I think the previous owners were hobbits,' Eve
said, determined to match his lightness.

He slumped down next to her on the sofa. 'The
hot water was fantastic while it lasted.'

Yeah. The water reservoir was pretty small. Even smaller as it ran through the onboard gas heater. 'Sorry about that. I guess Mr and Mrs Hobbit must have showered at different ends of the day.'

Not usually a problem for a woman travelling alone. The hot water was hers to use or abuse. And that had worked pretty well for her so far.

'So what's the plan for tonight?' Marshall said, glancing at her sideways.

Lord, if she wasn't fighting off visuals of him in the shower, she was hearing smut in every utterance. *Tonight*. It wasn't a very loaded word but somehow, in this tiny space with this über-present man, it took on piles of new meaning.

'Movie and bed—' She practically choked the word off.

But Marshall's full stomach and warm, fresh clothes had clearly put the damper on any lusty intentions. He didn't even blink. 'Sounds good. What have you got?'

Apparently an enormous case of the hormones, if her prickling flesh and fluttery tummy were any indication. But she nodded towards one of the drawers on the opposite side of the bus and left him to pick his way through the DVD choices. The mere act of him increasing the physical distance helped dilute the awareness that swirled around them.

He squatted and rifled through the box, revealing a stretch of brown, even skin at his lower back to taunt her. 'Got a preference?'

'No.'

Yeah. She'd have preferred never to have said yes to this excruciating co-habitation arrangement, to be honest. But done was done. She filled her one wineglass high for Marshall and then poured filtered water into her own mug where he couldn't tell what she was drinking. Maybe if he was sedated, that powerful, pulsing thrum coming off him would ease off a bit.

And maybe if she kept her wits about her she'd have the strength to resist it.

He held up a favourite. 'Speaking of hobbits...'

Yes! Something actiony and not at all romantic. He popped the disc at her enthusiastic nod, then settled back and jumped through the opening credits to get straight into the movie. Maybe he was as eager as she was to avoid conversation.

It took about ten minutes for her to remember that Middle Earth was definitely *not* without romance and then the whole movie became about the awkwardness of the longing-filled screen kiss that was swiftly approaching. Which only reminded her of how robbed she'd felt out in that cove to have the press of Marshall's lips snatched away by the approach of the *Vista II*.

Which was a ridiculous thing to be thinking when she should be watching the movie.

Hobbits quested. Wraiths hunted. Dramatic elven horse chase. Into the forests of Rivendell and then—

'Are we in the clunk zone, Eve?' Marshall suddenly queried. She flicked her eyes to her left and encountered his, all rust-flecked and serious and steady.

'What?'

Which was Eve-ish for *Yes...yes, we are.*

'Did I stuff things up this afternoon by kissing you?'

'You didn't kiss me,' she managed to squeeze out through her suddenly dry mouth.

But that gaze didn't waver. 'Not for want of trying.'

A waft of air managed to suck down into her lungs. 'Well, the moment has passed now so I think we're cool.'

'Passed?' he asked without smiling. 'Really?'

Yeah... She was a liar.

'That was hours ago,' she croaked.

'I wouldn't know,' he murmured. 'Time does weird things when you're around.'

Her brain wanted to laugh aloud, but the fluttering creatures inside her twittered girlishly with excitement. And they had the numbers.

'I think you're being adversely affected by the movie,' she said, to be safe.

'I'm definitely affected by something.'

'The wine?'

His smile was as gorgeous as it was slow. 'It is pretty good.'

'The company?'

'Yeah. 'Cos that's been terrific.'

She let her breath out in a long, apologetic hiss. 'I'm being weird.'

'You're weird so often it's starting to feel normal.'

'It's not awkward for you?'

His large hand slid up to brush a strand of hair from across her lips. 'What I'm feeling is not awkwardness.'

There went the whole dry mouth thing again. 'What are you feeling?'

'Anticipation.'

The fantastical world on-screen might as well have been an infomercial for all the attraction it suddenly held. Their already confined surroundings shrank even further.

'Maybe the moment's gone,' she said bravely.

He didn't move. He didn't have to. His body heat

reached out and brushed her skin for him. 'Maybe you're in denial.'

'You think I'm that susceptible to low lighting and a romantic movie?'

Sure enough, there was a whole lot of elven-human longing going on on-screen. Longing and whispering against an intimate, beautiful soundtrack. Seriously, why hadn't she insisted on something with guns?

'I think the movie was an admirable attempt.'

'At what?' she whispered.

'At not doing this…'

Marshall twisted himself upright, his fingers finding a safe haven for his nearly empty wineglass. His other hand simultaneously relieved her of her mug and reached past her to place it on the sideboard. It legitimised the sudden, closer press of his body into hers.

'Now,' he breathed, 'what were you about to say?'

Heat and dizziness swilled around her and washed all sense out to sea. 'When?'

'Back in the cove. Was it no?' Grey promise rained down on her. 'Or was it yes?'

Truly? She had to find the courage to do this again? It had been hard enough the first time. Though, somehow, having already confessed her feelings made it easier now to admit the truth. She took the deepest of breaths, just in case it was also her last.

'It wasn't no.'

Those beautiful lips twisted in a confident, utterly masculine smile. 'Good.'

And then they found hers. Hot and hard and yet exquisitely soft. Pressing into her, bonding them together, challenging her to respond. She didn't at first because the sensation of being kissed after so very long with no touch at all threw her mind into a state of befuddlement. And she was drowning pleasantly in the sensation of hard male body pressed against hers. And sinking into the clean, delicious taste of him.

But she'd always been a sure adaptor and it only took moments for her feet to touch bottom and push off again for the bright, glittery surface. Her hands crept up around Marshall's shoulder and nape, fusing them closer. Her chin tilted to better fit the angle of his lips. The humid scorch of his breath teased and tormented and roused her, shamefully.

Revived her.

God, she'd missed hot breath mingling with hers. Someone else's saliva in her mouth, the chemical rush that came with that. Tangling tongues. Sliding teeth. And not just any tongue, breath and teeth but ones that belonged with all that hard flesh and ink and leather.

Marshall's.

'You taste of wine, Weatherman,' she breathed.

His eyes fixated on her tongue as she savoured the extra flavour on her lips. 'Maybe it's your own?'

'I had water.'

He lifted back slightly and squinted at her. 'Trying to get me drunk?'

'Trying to fight the inevitable.'

His chuckle rumbled against her chest. 'How's that working out for you?'

Gentle and easy and undemanding and just fine with something as casual as she needed. Wanted. All that she could offer.

And so she gave him access—tempting him with the touch of her tongue—and the very act was a kind of psychological capitulation. Her decision made. Even before she knew she was making it.

She trusted Marshall, even if she didn't know him all that well. He'd been careful and understanding and honest, and her body was *thrumming* its interest in having more access to his. With very little effort she could have his bare, hot skin against hers and her fingertips buried in the sexy curve of all that muscle.

He was gorgeous. He was intriguing. He was male

and he was right here in front of her in living, breathing flesh and blood. And he was offering her what she suspected would be a really, really good time.

Did the rest really matter?

One large, hot hand slid up under her T-shirt and curled around her ribcage below her breast as they kissed, monitoring the heart rate that communicated in living braille onto his palm. Letting her get used to him being there. Doing to her exactly what she longed to do to him. Letting her stop him if she wanted. But no matter how many ways he twisted against her, the two of them couldn't get comfortable on the narrow little sofa. No wonder he'd struggled to sleep on it last night. And all the while she had an expansive bed littered with cloud-like pillows just metres away.

Eve levered herself off the sofa, not breaking contact with Marshall's lips or talented hands as he also rose, and she stretched as he straightened to his full height.

'Bed,' she murmured against his teeth.

His escalating kisses seemed to concur. One large foot bumped into hers and nudged it backwards, then another and the first one again. Like some kind of clunky slow dance, they worked their way back through the little kitchen, then through the en suite bathroom and toward unchartered territory. Her darkened bedroom. All the time, Marshall bonded them together either with his lips or his eyes or the hands speared into her hair and curled around her bottom.

There was something delightfully complicit about the way he used his body to steer her backwards into the bedroom while she practically tugged him after her. It said they were equals in this. That they were both accountable and that they both wanted it to happen.

Below her socked feet, the harder external floor of the en suite bathroom gave way to the plush carpet of the bedroom. Marshall's hands slid up to frame her face, holding it steady for the worship of his mouth. His tongue explored the welcome, warm place beyond her teeth just as much as she wanted him to explore this unchartered place beyond the doorway threshold.

A gentle fibrillation set up in the muscles of her legs, begging her to sink backwards onto her bed. The idea of him following her down onto it only weakened them further.

'Eve...' he murmured, but she ignored him, pulling back just slightly to keep the bedward momentum up. It took a moment for the cooler air of the gap she created to register.

Her eyes drifted open. They dropped to his feet,

which had stopped, toes on the line between carpet and timber boards.

Hard on the line.

Confusion brought her gaze back up to his.

'I don't expect this,' he whispered, easing the words with a soft brush of his lips. And, when she just blinked at him, his eyes drifted briefly to the bed in case she was too passion-dazzled to comprehend him.

She pulled again.

But those feet didn't shift from the line and so all she achieved was more space between them. Such disappointing, chilly space. At least the hot grasp of his hand still linked them.

'Marshall...?'

'I just wanted to kiss you.'

Ditto! 'We can kiss in here. More comfortably.'

But the distance was official now and tugging any more reeked of desperation so she grudgingly let his hand drop.

'If I get on that bed with you we won't just be kissing,' he explained, visibly moderating his breathing.

'And that's a problem because...?'

'This isn't some roadhouse.'

Confusion swelled up around her numb brain. 'What?'

'You don't strike me as the sex-on-the-first-date type.'

Really? There was a type for these things? 'I don't believe in types. Only circumstances.'

'Are you saying you're just up for it because it's convenient?'

Up for it. Well, that sucked a little of the romance out of things. Then again, romance was not why she'd put her tongue in his mouth just minutes ago. What she wanted from Marshall was what he'd been unconsciously promising her from the moment they'd met.

No strings.

No rules.

No consequences.

'I'm tired of being alone, Marshall. I'm tired of not feeling anything but sadness. I need to feel something good.' A guarded wariness stole over his flushed face and she realised she needed to give him more than that. 'I have no illusions that it's going to go anywhere; in fact, I need it to be short. I don't want the distraction.'

He still didn't look convinced.

'I haven't so much as touched another human being in months, Marshall.'

'Any port in a storm, then?'

God knew it would be stormy between them. As

wild and tempestuous as any sea squall. And just as brief.

'We've covered a lot of ground in our few days together and I trust you. I'm attracted to you. I need *you*, Marshall.'

All kinds of shapes seemed to flicker across the back of his intense gaze.

'But I'm not about to beg. Either you want me or you don't. I'll sleep comfortably tonight either way.' *Such lies!* 'Can you say the same?'

Of course he wanted her. It was written in the heave of his chest and the tightness of his muscles and the very careful way he wasn't making a single unplanned move. He wanted what she was offering, too, but there was something about it that he didn't want. Just...something.

And something was enough.

Eve went to push past him, back to the movie, making the disappointing decision for both of them.

But, as she did, his body blocked her path and his left foot crossed onto carpet. Then his right, backing her towards the bed. And then he closed the door on the sword fights of Middle Earth and plunged them into darkness, leaving only the smells and sounds and tastes of passion between them.

CHAPTER SEVEN

EVERY MUSCLE IN Eve's body twinged when she tried to move. Not that she could move particularly far with the heavy heat of Marshall's arm weighing her down. But in case she somehow managed to forget how the two of them had passed the long night, her body was there to remind her. In graphic detail.

Languid smugness glugged through her whole system.

She gave up trying to softly wiggle out of captivity and just accepted her fate. After all, there were much worse ways to go. And to wake up. Right now, her brain was still offering spontaneous flashbacks to specific moments of greatness between them last night, and every memory came with a sensation echo.

Beside her, Marshall slept on in all his insensible glory. Buried face first in her pillows, relaxed, untroubled. It was very tempting just to lie here until lunchtime committing Sleeping Beauty to memory.

Although there was her bladder…

Ugh.

She took more decisive action and slid Marshall's arm off her chest, which roused him sufficiently to croak as she sprang to her feet. 'Morning.'

When was the last time she'd *sprung* anywhere? Usually she just hauled herself out of bed and gritted her teeth as she got on with the business of living.

'Morning yourself. Just give me a sec.'

Easing her bladder just a couple of metres and a very thin en suite bathroom wall away from Marshall was an unexpectedly awkward moment. It seemed ridiculous after everything they'd shared in the past twelve hours to have to concentrate her way through a sudden case of bashful bladder. As soon as she was done and washed, she scampered back into the toasty warm and semi-occupied bed.

'You're better than an electric blanket,' she sighed, letting the heat soak into her cold feet.

'Feel free to snuggle in.'

Don't mind if I do. She was going to milk this one-night stand for every moment she could.

Marshall hauled her closer with the same strong arm that had held her captive earlier, her back to his chest in a pretty respectable spoon.

His voice rumbled down her spine. 'How are you feeling?'

Wow. Not an easy question to answer, and not one

she'd expected him to ask. That was a very *not* one-night stand kind of question. Thank goodness she wasn't facing him.

'I'm…' What was she? Elated? Reborn? She couldn't say that aloud. 'I have no regrets. Last night was absolutely what I expected and needed. And more. It was amazing, Marshall.'

It was only then that she realised how taut the body behind her had become. Awkwardness saturated his words when they eventually came.

'Actually, I meant because of today.'

She blinked. 'What's today?'

'One year?'

A bucket of icy Southern Ocean couldn't have been more effective. The frigid wash chased all the warmth of Marshall's hold away and left her aching and numb. And barely breathing.

Travis. Her poor, lost brother. Twelve months without a boy she'd loved her whole life and she'd let herself be distracted by a man she'd known mere moments by comparison.

She struggled for liberty and Marshall let her tumble out of bed to her feet.

'I'm fine,' she said tightly. 'Just another day.'

He pushed onto his side, giving her a ringside seat for the giant raptor on his chest. She'd so badly wanted to see it last night but the room was too dark. And now she was too gutted to enjoy it.

'Okay...'

Mortification soaked in. What was wrong with her? How much worse to know that, for those first precious moments of consciousness, she hadn't even remembered she *had* a brother. She'd been all about Marshall.

What kind of a sister was she, anyway?

You wanted to forget, that little voice inside reminded her cruelly. *Just for one night. Wasn't that the point?*

Yes. But not like this. Not entirely.

She hadn't meant to *erase* Travis.

'It's a number,' she lied, rummaging in a drawer before dragging on panties and then leggings.

'A significant one,' Marshall corrected quietly.

She pulled a comfortable sweater on over the leggings. 'It's not like it took me by surprise. I've been anticipating it.'

Marshall sat up against the bed head and tucked the covers up around his waist ultra-carefully. 'I know.'

'So why are you making it into an issue?'

Ugh... Listen to herself...

Storm-grey eyes regarded her steadily. 'I just

wanted to see how you were feeling this morning. Forget I mentioned it. You seem…great.'

The lie was as ridiculous as it was obvious.

'Okay.'

What was wrong with her? It wasn't Marshall's fault that she'd sought to use him for a bit of escapism. He'd fulfilled his purpose well.

Maybe too well.

'So, should we get going right after breakfast?' she asked brightly from the en suite bathroom as she brushed her hair. Hard to know whether all that heat in her cheeks was residual passion from last night, anger at herself for forgetting today or embarrassment at behaving like a neurotic teen.

Or all of the above.

A long pause from the bed followed and she slowed the drag of the bristles through her hair until it stilled in her hand.

'I've got to get back on the road,' she added, for something to fill the silence.

She should never have left it, really. She replaced the brush and then turned to stand in the bathroom doorway. Trying to be grown up about this. 'We both have jobs to do.'

What was going on behind that careful masculine expression? It was impossible to know. He even seemed to blink in slow motion. But his head eventually inclined—just.

'I'll convoy as far as the South Coast Highway,' he started. 'Then I'll head back to Kal. The road should be open by now.'

Right.

Was that disappointment washing through her midsection? Did she imagine that last night would have changed anything? She *wanted* them to go their separate ways. She'd practically shouted at him that this was a one-off thing. Yet bitterness still managed to fight its way through all her self-pity about Travis.

'Yeah. Okay.'

That was probably for the best. Definitely.

'Do you want me to take some posters for the Norseman to Kalgoorlie stretch? That'll save you doubling back down the track.'

It physically hurt that he could still be considerate when she was being a jerk. A twinge bit deep in her chest and she had to push words through it. Her shoulder met the doorframe.

'You're a nice man, Marshall Sullivan.'

His blankness didn't alter. And neither did he move. 'So I've been told.'

Then nothing. For ages. They just stared at each other warily.

Eventually he went to fling back the covers and

Eve spun on the spot before having to face the visual temptation of everything she'd explored with her fingers and lips last night, and made the first excuse she could think of.

'I'll get some toast happening.'

Nice.

Just what every man wanted to hear from a woman he'd spent the night with. Not 'fantastic' or 'unforgettable'. Not 'awe-inspiring' or 'magnificent'.

Nice.

He'd heard that before, from the Sydney kids who had clambered over him in their quest to get closer to Rick and his chemical smorgasbord. From friends and girls and the occasional tragic teacher.

He'd always been the *nicer* brother.

But not the one everyone wanted access to.

Sticks and stones…

Problem was, Eve's lips might have been issuing polite compliments but the rest of her was screaming eviction orders and, though he'd only known her a couple of days, it was long enough for him to recognise the difference. He'd had enough one-off encounters with women to know *get out of my room* when he saw it. Despite all the brave talk last night, she was *not* comfortable with the aftermath of their exhausting night together.

And he was all too familiar with eyes that said something different from words. He'd had them all his life.

He'd been right in assuming Eve wasn't a woman who did this a lot; she was most definitely under-rehearsed in the fine art of the morning-after kiss-off. If he'd realised there'd be no lingering kisses this morning he would have taken greater care to kiss her again last night just before they fell into an exhausted slumber twisted up in each other.

Because Eve had just made it very clear that there would be no more kissing between them.

Ever.

He'd worked his butt off last night giving her the kind of night she clearly needed from him. Making sure it was memorable. And, if he was honest, giving Eve something to think about. To regret. Maybe that was why it stung even more to see her giving it exactly zero thought this chilly morning.

Wham-bam, thank you, Marshall.

Somewhere, the universe chuckled to itself as the cosmic balance evened up. That was what he got for usually hotfooting it out the next morning the way Eve just had.

Only generally to fire up his motorcycle, not the toaster.

What did he expect? Days wrapped up in each other's arms here in this ridiculous little bus while his remaining weeks on the project ticked ever closer to an end and her bank balance slowly drained away? Neither of them had the luxury of indefinite leisure. He wasn't stupid.

Or maybe he was…because Evelyn Read was definitely not a one-off kind of woman and some deep part of him had definitely hoped for more than the single night they'd both agreed on between kisses. Which meant it was probably just as well that was all he was getting. Eve had no room for another man in her single-track life.

And he was done being a means to an end.

He pulled yesterday's T-shirt back on and rather enjoyed the rumples and creases. They were like little trophies. A reminder of how the shirt had been thoroughly trampled underfoot in their haste to get each other naked. A souvenir of the disturbingly good time he'd had with her beyond her bedroom door.

'Don't burn it,' he murmured, passing into the tiny kitchenette intentionally close to her, just to get one more feel of her soft skin. His body brushed the back of hers.

Her feet just about left the floor, she jumped that fast and high. Then a sweet heat coloured along her jawline and her lips parted and he had to curl his fingers to stop himself from taking her by the hand and dragging her back to that big, warm bed and reminding her what lips were made for.

It felt good to torture Eve, just a little bit. It sure felt good to surprise her into showing her hand like that. To shake the ambivalence loose. To watch the unsteadiness of her step. She might call a halt to this thing just getting going between them but he wasn't going to go easily.

He kept on moving past her, ignoring the sweet little catch in her breath, and he stopped at the back doors, flung them open and then stretched his hands high to hook them on the top of the bus, stretching out the kinks of the night, knowing how his back muscles would be flexing. Knowing how the ink there would flash from beneath his T-shirt. Knowing how that ink fascinated her.

If she was going to drive off into the horizon this morning, she sure wasn't going to do it with a steady brake foot.

Yup. He was a jerk.

He leapt down from the bus and turned to his KTM, and murmured to the bitter cold morning.

'*Nice*, my ass.'

The bus's brake lights lit up on the approach to the junction between the Coolgardie and South Coast

Highways and Marshall realised he hadn't really thought this through. It was a big intersection but not built for pulling over and undertaking lingering farewells. It was built for turning off in any of the four points of the compass. His road went north, Eve's went further west.

But the uncertain blink of her brake lights meant she, too, was hesitating on the pedal.

She didn't know what to do either.

Marshall gave the KTM some juice and pulled up in the turn lane beside her instead, reassuring himself in the mirror that there was no one on the remote highway behind them. Eve dropped her window as he flipped his helmet visor.

'Good luck with the rest of your trip,' he called over the top of his thrumming engine and her rattling one.

'Thank you.' It was more mouthed than spoken.

God, this was a horrible way of doing this. 'I hope you get some news of your brother soon.'

Eve just nodded.

Then there was nothing much more to say. What could he say? So he just gave her a small salute and went to lower his visor. But, at the last moment, he found inspiration. 'Thank you for coming with me yesterday. I know you would have rather been back on the road.'

Which was code for *Thanks for last night, Eve*. If only he were the slightest bit emotionally mature.

She nodded again. 'I'm glad I did it.'

Middle Island, he told himself. Yesterday. That was all.

And then a car appeared on the highway in his mirror, way back in the distance, and he knew they were done.

He saluted again, slid his tinted visor with the obligatory squished bugs down between them and gave the bike some juice. It took only seconds to open up two hundred metres of highway between them and he kept Eve in his mirrors until the Bedford crossed the highway intersection and was gone from view, heading west.

Not the worst morning-after he'd ever participated in, but definitely not the best.

He was easily the flattest he could remember being.

He hadn't left his number. Or asked for hers. Neither of them had volunteered it and that was telling. And, without a contact, they'd never find each other again, even if they wanted to.

Eve Read would just have to be one of those memories he filed away deep inside. He added *The Crusader* to his list of badly handled flings.

Except she didn't feel like a fling. She felt like forever. Or what he imagined forever must feel like. Crazy. He'd known her all of five minutes. So the lingering sense that things weren't done between them was…

Ridiculous.

The shimmering haze of her exhaust as she couldn't speed away from him fast enough told a very different story.

Trees and wire fences and road signs whizzed by the KTM in a one-hundred-and-ten-kilometre-per-hour blur. Plus a sheep or two.

Would he have stayed if she'd asked? If she'd crawled back into bed this morning and snuggled in instead of running an emotional mile? If he hadn't—like a freaking genius—brought up her most painful memory when she was half-asleep and vulnerable to his words?

Yeah. He would have stayed.

But it was the *why* that had him by the throat.

Eve was pretty but not beautiful, bright but not spectacular, prickly as a cactus and more than a little bit neurotic. She should have just been a charming puzzle. So what was with the whole curl-up-in-bed urge? He really wasn't the curl up type.

She's your damsel, man.

The words came burbling up from deep inside him, in his brother's voice. The kind of conversations they used to have way back when. Before they went down opposite off ramps of the values highway. Before Rick's thriving entrepreneurial phase. Certainly before Christine switched teams—and brothers. Back when Rick gave him stick for being a soft touch for girls in need of a knight on a white charger.

Orange charger, in his case.

Relief surfed his veins.

Yeah, this was about Eve's brother. That was all it was, this vague sense that leaving her was wrong. There was nothing more meaningful or complicated going on than that. He hated the helplessness he saw behind Eve's eyes and the flat nothing she carried around with her. It made him feel powerless—his least favourite emotion.

She's not yours to fix, Inner Rick nudged.

No, but was there really nothing more he could offer her than platitudes and some help with the posters and one night of sweaty distraction? He was a resourceful guy. He had connections.

And then it hit him…

Exactly why he'd chosen to place a woman he'd just met and a man he hadn't seen in ten years next to each other at the dinner table of his subconscious.

His brain ticked over as fast as his tyres ate up the highway. If a person was going to go off grid, they might ditch their bank accounts in favour of cash, stop filing tax returns and opt out of claiming against Medicare. But what was Eve the most cut up about—? That Travis was struggling with his panic disorder, alone. And what did people who were being treated for disorders do? They took drugs. And who knew everything there was to know about drugs?

Rick did.

Enough to have driven his kid brother away years before. Enough to have made a thriving business out of supplying half of Sydney with their chemical needs. Enough to have a world of dodgy contacts inside the pharmaceutical industry—legal and otherwise.

Marshall eased off the throttle.

That meant he was just one uncomfortable phone call away from the kind of information that the cops would never think to access. Or be able to. Not ethical, probably not even legal, but since when did Rick let something as insignificant as the law stand between him and his goals?

Of course it would mean speaking to his brother, but maybe a decade was long enough with the silent treatment. Lord knew, Rick owed him.

Marshall down-geared and, as he did, his rapid pulse started to slow along with his bike. The pulse that had kicked up the moment parting from Eve was upon him. Back at the intersection. A kind of anxiety that he hadn't felt in a long, long time—since before he'd stopped letting himself care for people.

The descending thrum of his blood and the guttural throb of his bike colluded to soak him in a kind of certainty about this plan. As if it was somehow cosmically meant to be. As if maybe this was why he'd met Eve in the first place.

Because he could help her.

Because he could save her.

That was all this was. This…unsettling obsession. It was his Galahad tendency. Evelyn Read needed *help*, not *him*. And he was much more comfortable with the helping part.

He hit his indicator and looked for a safe place to pull over. He fished around in the depths of his wallet for a scrap of paper he'd almost forgotten he still carried. Ratty and brown edged, the writing half-faded. Rick's phone number. He punched the number into his phone but stopped short of pressing Dial.

This was Rick. The brother who'd made his teenage years a living hell. Who'd lured his girlfriend away from him just because he could. The brother who'd been the real reason that most of his friends craved his company and half the teachers gave him special treatment. They'd all wanted an in with *The Pharmacist*.

Rick was the reason he couldn't bring himself to trust a single soul, even now. Rick had taken the lessons they'd both learned from their mother about love and loyalty—or absences thereof—and turned the hurt into a thriving new industry where a lack of compassion for others was a corporate asset.

He'd made it work for him, while his little brother struggled in his shadow.

It had taken him years to fortify himself against those early lessons. His mother's. His brother's. And here he was, straddling his bike and contemplating leaping off the edge of his personal fortress of solitude to help someone he barely knew. He'd kicked the door of communication closed between every part of his old life and here he was, poised to take to that door with a crowbar and crack it open again. For a virtual stranger.

No...*for Eve*.

And Eve mattered.

He thumbed the dial button and listened as the number chirped its ominous melody. Took three deep breaths as it rang and rang. Took one more as a gruff voice picked up.

Marshall didn't waste time with niceties.

'You said to call if I ever needed you,' he reminded his brother. 'Did you mean it…?'

Rick had been at first surprised, then wary, when he recognised Marshall's serious tone after so very long. But—typical of the brother he remembered—Rick took the call at face value and accepted the subtext without comment. He listened to the request, grizzled about the dubiousness of what he'd been asked to do, but committed to help. And, despite anything else he'd done in his life, Rick Sullivan was the personification of tenacity. If he said he'd get this done, then, one way or another, some time Marshall's phone would be ringing again.

End of day, that was all that really mattered. Eve needed results more than he needed to maintain the moral high ground.

Rick even managed to go the entire phone call without getting personal.

The leathers of Marshall's jacket creaked as he exhaled. 'Thank you for your help, Rick. I swear it's not for anything too dodgy.'

'This whole thing is dodgy,' his brother muttered. 'But I'll do it because it's you. And because dodgy is where I do my best work. It might take a while, though.'

'No problem.'

Eve had been waiting twelve months. What was one more?

'I might find nothing.'

'Understood.'

'And one day maybe you can tell me what we're doing. And who for.'

He tensed up, mostly at the suggestion that there'd be a 'one day'. As if the door couldn't be closed once jemmied open.

'What makes you think there's a "who"?'

'Because you don't get invested in things, brother. Ever. You're Mr Arm's Length. But I can hear it in your voice. This matters.'

'Just let me know how you go,' he muttered. Eve was not someone he would trust his brother with, even mentally. He wasn't about to share any details.

'So…you want to know whether she's okay?' Rick asked, just before they ended the call.

'Christine?' Speaking of not trusting Rick… A few years ago, he would have felt the residual hurt deep in his gut. But now it just fluttered to earth like a burnt ember. Maybe the history really was history now.

'No, not Christine. I have no idea where she ended up.'

That bit. That Rick hadn't even kept his prize after working so very hard to take it from him.

'I meant Mum,' Rick clarified. 'Remember her?'

Everything locked up tight inside Marshall. He'd closed the door on Laura Sullivan the same day he'd locked Rick out of his life. The two of them were a package deal. The moment she'd realised her enterprising oldest son was going to be a far better provider than the Government, she'd made her allegiance—and her preference—totally clear.

That wasn't something you forgot in a hurry… Your own mother telling you to go.

'No. I'm good.'

There didn't seem much else to say after that.

It took just a moment to wind the call up and slip his phone back into his pocket. He'd get a new number just as soon as Rick gave him the info he needed. But he didn't hit the road again straight away. Instead, he sat there on the highway, bestride his KTM, breathing out the tension.

You don't get invested in things.

Well, that pretty much summed him up. Work. Life. He had a good ethic but he never let himself care. Because caring was a sure way of being disappointed. Or hurt. Life in his brother's shadow had taught him that. And as life lessons went, that one had served him well.

Until now.

As Rick had readily pointed out, he was invested

now. With Eve—a woman he barely knew. He was more intrigued and conflicted and turned inside out for a woman he'd known just days than the people he'd grown up with. Maybe because she didn't want anything from him that she wasn't prepared to own. She had no agenda. And no ulterior motive.

Eve just…was.

And maybe he'd found a way to help her. Or maybe not. But he sure wasn't going to be able to do it from here.

He'd just sent her off down the highway with absolutely no way of locating her again. No email. No number. No forwarding address. How many Reads might there be in Melbourne? He couldn't shake the screaming thought that this was the only moment he had left. Right now, Eve was rattling down a long, straight road that only went to one place. After that, she could head off in any of five different routes into tourist country and his chances of finding her would evaporate. Tension coiled inside him like a spring…

And that was when he knew.

This wasn't just about helping Eve. If it was, he could just take whatever information his brother dug up straight to the authorities. Let them do the rest. This wasn't just about some cosmic interference to help her find her brother. That unfamiliar, breath-stealing tightness in his chest was panic. And he didn't do panic because that implied caring.

He'd no sooner let himself care for someone than void a ten-year stalemate with his criminal brother to get something that might ease Eve's pain. Eve—a complex, brittle, single-minded angel. The most intriguing woman he'd met in…more than years. The woman who'd barrelled through his defences and wedged herself there between his ribs. Just below his heart.

Oh, crap…

From where he sat, he could see the endless stretch of highway ahead—north to Kalgoorlie, where he could pick up his work trail where he'd left it a few days ago. But, in his mirror, he could see the long straight run behind him, back to the four-way turn-off. Back to a one hundred per cent chance of catching up with the bus before it turned off the western highway.

Back to the possibility he'd been too cowardly to explore.

Back to Eve.

He started his engine, dropped his visor and let his eyes lift to the northern horizon. Towards work and the conclusion of this trip and his safe, comfortable life.

But then they dropped again to the mirror, and the road he'd just travelled.

Sure, she might tell him to get lost. And if she did, he would.

But what if she didn't…?

In the end, his hands made the decision before his head did, and a leathered thumb hit his indicator before pulling the KTM's handlebars right, out across the empty highway and then back onto the opposite shoulder.

Before he could second-guess himself, he gunned the accelerator and roared off towards the south.

Towards the unknown.

CHAPTER EIGHT

IT COULD BE ANYONE—that speck in the distance behind her.

Car. Bike. Truck. It was too small for one of the massive road trains that liked to thunder past at breakneck speed, but a smaller truck, maybe.

Eve forced her eyes forward and ignored the impulse to check again. Plenty of people drove this road into Western Australia's tourist region. People who had far more legitimate reasons to be heading this way than *he* did.

Marshall was heading north. Back to his weather stations. Back to reality.

Which was exactly what she should be doing. Middle Island had been a nice couple of days of escapism—for both of them—but they both had jobs to be doing.

And Travis was her job.

He always had been.

If the past couple of days had taught her anything, it was that she couldn't take her eyes off the prize—

or the map—for a moment. Look how fast she'd been swayed from her purpose. Besides, Marshall couldn't get out of there fast enough this morning. Not once he saw her in full neurotic mode. He was probably congratulating himself right now on a bullet well dodged.

The speck in her rear-vision mirror grew larger. But not large enough to be a truck. A car, then.

Or smaller, her subconscious more than whispered.

No.

Why would Marshall return? He hadn't left anything behind in her bus—she'd checked twice. And their parting had been as unequivocal as it was awkward. And definitely for the best. She was on a mission and didn't need the distraction. No matter how compelling.

And boy, was he ever. He'd been an intriguing curiosity while tattooed and hairy. Clean shorn and well educated, he was entrancing. Naked, he was positively hypnotic. All the better for being a long, long way from her.

She glanced helplessly back at the mirror and her pulse made itself known against the fragile skin of her throat.

Not a car.

Her gaze split its time between looking ahead and

looking back, then the forward-looking part became a glance and then a mere flick to keep the bus on a straight and safe line.

Plenty of motorbikes in the sea. Impossible to even know what colour this one was yet.

Her gaze remained locked on her mirror.

If it was orange—if it was *him*—that didn't have to mean anything. Their one night together had probably been so good because it was a one-off. No past, no future. Just the very heated and very comfortable present. Even if Marshall was coming back for a second go at last night, there was nothing that said she had to oblige—no matter what her pulse recommended.

No matter how enticing the promise of a few more hours of mental *weightlessness* he brought.

A dull mass settled between her shoulder blades. She couldn't afford to be weightless. Not until her journey was complete and Travis was home.

Her own thought tripped her up. She'd never thought about this journey being over. What she would do. Would work have her back? She'd resigned with notice, so there were no burnt bridges there, but could she go back to meetings and minutes and deadlines? Would she have the patience? What would she be like after it was all over? Could she be *normal* now that she knew how secretly cruel the world really was?

As for weightless… Would she ever feel that way again?

Or was that just another disloyalty to Travis? To be worrying about any of it?

She'd put herself first once before and look how that had ended. Travis had melted down completely the moment she took her eyes off him.

She glanced up again, just in time to see a flash of black and orange changing into the inside lane and then roaring up beside her.

All the breath squeezed up tight in her suddenly constricted chest.

He was back.

Marshall whizzed by on her right, then changed lanes into the vanguard position and weaved in the lane in a kind of high-speed wave. She took several long, steadying breaths to bring the mad thump of her heart back into regular rhythm.

Should she stop? Hear what he had to say?

No. If he wanted her to pull over he'd be braking, slowing her. But he was pacing her, not slowing her. Guiding her onward. Besides, not far now until the turn-off to the Ravensthorpe poster drop. If he had something to say he could say it there.

And she'd listen politely and when it came to the

time to part again she'd try and be a bit more erudite than her poor effort this morning.

Two vehicles whizzed by in the opposite direction, marking their entry into tourist country. *Tourism.* That was what she and Marshall were doing, right? Exploring the unchartered country that was each other. Enjoying the novelty. But how many tourists sold up and moved to the places they visited? How many stayed forever? No matter how idyllic.

Right. Because the real world eventually intruded.

And her reality was Travis.

Marshall wiggled his motorbike again and seemed to be waiting for something. Did he seriously worry that she hadn't recognised him? She gave her headlights a quick flash of acknowledgement and his weaving ceased.

He placed himself squarely in the centre of their lanc and let his bike eat up the highway.

And Eve did her best not to fixate on the strong breadth of his back and breathless imaginings about what it would be like to peel all that leather right off him.

The Bedford's front doors were as reluctant to open as Eve was to pass through them. But Marshall had made fast work of slinging the KTM onto its stand and pulling off his helmet. As he sauntered towards her on his thick-soled riding boots, he forked fingers through his thick helmet hair to ruffle it up.

Her first thought—on the clench of her stomach—was that finger-forking his hair was her job.

Her second thought—on the clench of her heart at the sound and smell of his creaking leathers as he stopped in front of her—was that she was completely screwed.

'Forget something?' she managed to squeeze out from the top of the Bedford's steps. More for something to say, really, because if he'd actually come back for his favourite socks she was going to be really crushed. She kept her body language as relaxed as was possible in a body ready to flee.

'Yeah,' he murmured, stepping up onto the bottom step, 'this.'

One gloved hand came up and lifted her chin as if he was holding a crystal flute and his lips brushed against hers. Then the brush got harder, closer. So... *so* much better. He turned his head and deepened the kiss, stroking his tongue into her mouth and against her own. Just when she'd thought no one would ever kiss her like that again.

She wavered there on the top step, the closest thing to a swoon she'd ever experienced.

'I didn't say goodbye properly,' he finally breathed

against her astonished mouth. 'Now I don't want to say it at all.'

'You left,' she said between the head spins.

'But I'm back.'

'What about work?'

'What about it? There are plenty of weather stations still on my list. I'll just flex my route.'

What about my *work?* was what she really needed to be asking. Because how much of it was she going to get done with him around? If the past couple of days was any indication.

'You just assume I want to carry on where we left off?'

Just because she *did...* He wasn't to know that.

'I'm not assuming anything. If you send me away I've wasted...what...an hour of my time and a couple of bucks in fuel. Those are reasonable stakes.'

She pulled free. 'Charming.'

His grin managed to warm her right through, even as her heart screamed at her not to fall for it.

'Do you want me to go?'

She stared at him. Remembered how it felt to be with him. To be *with* him. And the thought of watching him drive off again was almost unbearable.

'I should,' she breathed.

'That's not a no.'

'No.' She stared at him. 'It's not.'

His puppy-dog grin graduated into a full, brilliant, blazing smile. 'Come on, then. Let's get some posters up. Time's a-wasting.'

He stepped down off the bus and held a hand out to help her. His eyes were screened by sunglasses but she could clearly see the trepidation still in the stiffness of his body. What she did next mattered to him. And that made her feel a whole lot better. She glanced at his outstretched hand. The unexpected chivalry excited and troubled her at the same time. She'd been jumping down off the Bedford's steps all by herself for eight months.

But just because she *could* didn't mean it wasn't a rare treat not to have to.

How would it feel to share this burden, just for a bit?

Would Travis understand?

After an age, she slid her bare fingers into his leathery ones and accepted his help.

But they both knew that taking his hand was saying yes to a whole lot more.

Marshall followed Eve as she chugged the Bedford into the biggest town in the Great Southern region behind the two-dozen cars that constituted peak hour in these parts. When she pulled up in a big open car park, Marshall stood the KTM and then jogged off to find something for them to eat. When he got back with it, she was set up and ready to go. Table and chair in place, bus sides up and covered in posters.

'I need to find the MP's office,' she announced. 'I'm getting low on posters.'

'Didn't you do that before?'

'Nope. Somebody distracted me.'

Yeah. He was probably supposed to feel bad about that. 'Too bad.' He winced.

'You don't look very sympathetic,' she admonished.

He just couldn't stop smiling. What was that about? 'MP's office was a few doors down from where I got lunch. I'll show you.'

Then it was her turn to smile. 'Thank you.'

She weighted down anything on her display that might blow away, grabbed a flash drive from her wallet and hurried alongside him. The door to the MP's office set off an audible alert as they entered.

'Hi there,' a friendly young woman said from behind the reception desk, addressing him. He looked straight at Eve, who slid the flash drive over the counter. 'Welcome to Albany.'

'Can you run off a hundred of these, please?'

The woman frowned and didn't touch the flash drive. 'What is it?'

'A missing-person poster,' Eve elucidated, but it didn't bring any hint of recognition. 'MP's offices are supposed to run off copies for free.'

A little explanation wasn't exactly an Open Sesame.

'Let me just check,' the woman said, stalling.

Eve looked as if she wanted to say more but his hand on her wrist forestalled it. A few moments later the woman came back, smiling, and chirped, 'Won't be long!'

Eve turned to the window and the port view beyond it and curled her arms around her torso.

Every day must have moments like these for her. When simple things like a bit of public bureaucracy suddenly reared up in front of her like a hurdle in her efforts to find her brother. No wonder she was so tired.

That kind of emotional ambush would be exhausting.

'Good morning,' a male voice said and Eve turned from her view.

An overly large, overly suited man with a politician's smile approached, hand outstretched. 'Gerald Harvey, MP.'

'Evelyn Read,' she murmured, sliding her fingers into his.

He followed suit. 'Marshall Sullivan.'

'You have a missing person?' the man asked and barrelled onwards before she could answer. 'I'm very sorry for your loss.'

'My loss?'

The statement seemed to stop Eve cold, and only the new colour in her face gave Gerald Harvey a hint that he might have put his finely shod foot in it. 'Your…uh…circumstances.'

Marshall stepped in closer behind her and placed his hand on Eve's lower back, stroking gently.

'Thank you,' she said to the man, more evenly than he would have expected based on her expression.

Harvey took the first poster that his assistant printed and read it aloud, rolling the name over his tongue like wine. 'Travis James Read.'

Just in case Eve didn't know who she'd been looking for the past year.

'Can't say I've seen him but someone might have. Are you circulating these in town?'

'All over the country.'

The man laughed. 'Not all over it, surely.'

Eve didn't waver. 'All over it. Every town. Every tourist stop.'

He stared as the poster in his hand fell limply over his substantial fist, and Marshall watched the interplay of disbelief and pity play over his ruddy face. Then it coalesced into kind condescension.

'That's a lot of posters.'

Brilliant. Of all the things he could have noted about Eve's extraordinary endeavour...

'Yes.'

'And fuel.'

Okay, enough was enough.

'Eve,' he interjected, 'how about we go back to the bus and I'll come back for the posters in fifteen minutes? You should get started. Don't want to miss anyone.'

Ironic, given her life was all about missing someone.

He thanked the MP and then bustled her out into the street, instantly feeling the absence of the tax payer–funded office heating. She didn't speak. Didn't confront him or rant. She'd turned inwards somewhere in that brief encounter and wasn't coming out any time soon.

He could endure the silence no longer than five minutes.

'Did I ever look at you like that?' he eventually asked as they walked back towards the main street. The mixture of pity and polite concern. As if she might not be all that mentally well herself.

His direct question dragged her focus back to him.

Brown eyes reached into his soul like a fist and twisted. 'A little bit.'

Great. No wonder she'd taken a while to warm up to him. Maybe she still was.

'It's not crazy,' he insisted suddenly, stopping and turning her towards him. 'It's not common, sure, but what you're doing is…logical. Under the circumstances. I get it.'

'You do?'

He waved his hand towards her poster display of all *The Missing* as they approached. 'I imagine every one of their families would like to have the courage and commitment to do what you've done. To get out here and look, personally. To do something proactive. To know you've done as much as you possibly can.'

She tossed her head back in the direction of the MP's office. 'That reaction is pretty common.'

'People don't know what to say, I guess.'

She stared up at him. 'You didn't have that problem.'

Something bloomed deep inside on learning that she had forgiven him for whatever first impression he'd left her with. Enough to shrug and joke, 'I'm exceptional.'

The sadness cracked and her mouth tipped up. 'So you say.'

'Go,' he nudged. 'Get started. I'll go back and manage Mr Charm, and then I'll go find us a camping site after I've dropped your new posters to you.'

She seemed to do a full-body sigh. 'Thank you.'

'No problem. Back in a few.'

He turned back for the MP's office but only got a few steps before turning again. He was back beside her in moments.

'Wha—?'

It took no effort at all to pull her into his arms and tuck her safe and warm beneath his chin. To wrap his arms firmly around her so that nothing and no one could get between them.

How had it not occurred to him before now to hug Eve?

This was a woman who needed repeat and regular hugging. On prescription. And he was happy to be her spoonful of sugar. Her slim arms crept around his waist and hooked behind his back, and the rest of her pressed into his chest as she sagged into him. Stroking her hair seemed obvious.

Around them, the sounds of a busy coastal town clattered on.

But inside their bubble there was only the two of them.

'That guy was a dick,' he announced against her ear.

'I know,' she muffled into his chest.

'I'm sorry that happened.'

She wriggled in closer. 'You get used to it.'

'You shouldn't have to.'

'Thank you.'

He curled her in closer, resting his chin on her head.

'Um…Marshall?' she eventually mumbled.

'Yeah?'

'Aren't you going to get us a site?'

'Yep. Leaving now.'

Around them traffic did its thing and somewhere a set of traffic lights rattled off their audible alert.

'Marshall?'

His fingers stroked her hair absently. 'Hmm?'

'We're making a scene.'

He opened one eye and, sure enough, a couple of locals walked by, glancing at them with amused smiles on their faces.

He closed the eye again and tucked her in even closer.

'Screw 'em.'

'Gotta say, you have a strange idea of what constitutes a "camping site".'

'I'm funded to stay in motels.' Marshall shrugged. 'You might as well benefit.'

'Are all your *motels* quite this flash?' She leaned

on the word purposefully because the waterside complex was more of a resort than anything.

'Well, no. But you put me up the last two nights so I have some budget savings. And there's hardly anyone else here out of season so you can take as much car park room as you need for the bus.'

Because she'd be sleeping in the car park while he spread out in the suite's big bed all alone?

She glanced at him. Maybe she'd misunderstood what his return meant. But she wasn't brave enough to ask aloud. Or maybe that was actually a really good idea. A tempestuous one-night stand was one thing but a second night—that needed some managing.

'Come on. At least check it out since you're here.'

She followed him up to the second storey, where the suite's balcony looked out over a parkland walkway below to the turquoise, pine tree–lined swimming bay that curled left and right of them. The rest of the suite was pretty much made of either sofa or bed. Both enormous. A large flat-screen TV adorned the walls between local art and something tantalising and white peeked out at her, reflected, through the bathroom door.

Her breath sucked in. Was that a…?

'Spa?'

'Yeah, I think so,' he said a little sheepishly. Had

it suddenly dawned on him that this was all starting to look a little *boom-chick-a-wah-wah*? 'It came with the room.'

How long had it been since she'd soaked her weary body? And having a spa, or lounging on the sofa, or sitting on the balcony with a glass of wine didn't have to mean she was staying the night here. Her own bed was pretty comfy, thanks very much.

She glanced at the crack in the bathroom door again and wondered how she could ask him for access without it sounding like a come-on. Or an invitation.

As usual, Marshall came to her rescue with the lift of one eloquent eyebrow and the careful and chivalrous choice of words.

'You want first crack?'

It took her about a nanosecond to answer in the positive and about two minutes to sprint back to the bus and get some clean clothes. It was only as she took the stairs back up two by two that she realised what the bundle of comfortable leggings and track top in her arms meant.

They weren't going back out again tonight.

So, that meant room service for dinner. Nice and cosy, just the two of them.

Wow. Her subconscious was really going to make

this tough for her. But the siren song of the bubbles was so strong she didn't care.

Bubbles. Heaven.

'It's a fast filler,' Marshall announced as she burst back into the room, more eager than she'd felt in a long time.

Oh, right…filling. Nature's brakes. Eve stood, a bit at a loss, shifting from foot to foot in the room's entryway.

'It has a shower, too,' he volunteered, bright light glinting in the grey of his eyes. 'You could get straight in and then just shower until the water level is high enough.'

She loved her bus, but its shower pressure was as weak as it was brief. The chance for a proper shower was overwhelming. 'Oh, my gosh, really?'

'Your face is priceless.' He grinned. 'You like a spa, I take it.'

'I used to have a jet bath,' Eve admitted to him. And then to herself, 'I miss it.'

Not that she'd given her big four-person bath much thought when she put her house on the market. Because brothers before bubbles, right? But—oh—how she missed the great soak at the end of a long, hard week. And out here where every week was long and hard…

'Go on,' he nudged. 'Get in there.'

Her thanks were practically a squeak as she slipped into the bathroom and closed the door behind her. She waited a moment too long to flip the lock—worrying how Marshall might read the click after such a long, silent pause—but decided to leave it. If he had something nefarious in mind, he'd had plenty of more isolated opportunities to perpetrate his crime. Not to mention the fact they'd already slept together.

Besides, sneaking into a woman's bathroom was beneath a man like Marshall.

He's a good man.

It took no time at all to get naked and under the thundering commercial shower as the water slowly rose up over her calves. Hot, hot water pounded down on her shoulders and back, then over her hair as she plunged fully under it.

Warm and reassuring and…home. The water brought with it a full-body rush of tingles.

Unexpected tears rushed to her support.

She'd been doing this so long. Being on the road. Was it okay to admit she was tired? That didn't have to mean she loved Travis any less, did it? The water thundered on and she lifted her face to let the fresh water wash away her guilty tears. Eventually, though, the spa reached a generous level of fullness and she killed the overhead stream and slid down into the piping-hot pool. Her groan was inevitable and the long sigh that followed the perfect punctuation.

When was the last time she'd felt so…buoyant? When was the last time she'd just closed her eyes and floated? The water's heat did its job and immediately soaked into muscles she'd forgotten didn't always feel this way, including a few that had only been aching since the marathon of last night.

Was it only twenty-four hours ago that she and Marshall had twisted up in each other's arms? And legs. And tongues. Like some kind of fantasy. Had it even really happened? If it had really happened, wouldn't he be in here with her? Not respectfully waiting on the other side of a closed—but not locked—door.

She lifted one hand to better position it and the cascading tinkle echoed in the silent bathroom.

'Marshall…'

'Yeah?'

Water splashed slightly as she started in the bath at the speed and closeness with which he answered. The door was right next to her head but he sounded close enough to be in here with her. Her eyes went to the mirror reflection of the door instinctively, but she knew before they got there what they'd find.

Marshall wasn't really the Peeping Tom type. If he

wanted to look, he'd just knock and enter and stare at her until she was as much a hot puddle as the spa water around her.

Because he's a good man, and he knows what he wants.

So what was he doing? Just lurking there? Or did the suite have some kind of weird acoustic thing going on?

She cleared her throat gently. 'Are you busy?'

'Nope. Just unwinding.' Pause. 'Why?'

'I just thought…maybe we could talk.'

'Didn't you want to relax?'

'It's a bit…quiet.'

'I thought you'd be used to that after eight months on the road.'

Yeah. He had a point. Astonishing what two days of company did for a girl.

'Normally I'd have music in my bathroom.' Classical. Mellow.

That deep voice was rich with humour. 'You want me to sing something?'

The very idea added to her hot-water tingles. 'Talking will be fine.'

'Okay.' Another pause. 'What do you want to talk about?'

'I don't know. Where you grew up? Your family? Anything, really.'

The door gave a muffled rattle and Eve wondered if he'd leaned on it. She took the complimentary sponge from its packet and filled it with warm water, then squeezed it down her arms.

Rinse. Repeat.

The slow splashes filled the long silence and the steam started working on her pores. And her soul.

'I'm not sure my history will be particularly conducive to relaxation.'

The tightness in his voice paused her sponge midswab. 'Really, why?'

'My family's about as functional as yours.'

Dead, drunken mother and AWOL brother was going to be tough to top. But her curiosity was piqued. 'Where are they now?'

'They're still in Sydney.'

'That doesn't sound so very dramatic.'

'Growing up had…its challenges.'

Her sponging resumed. Eve closed her eyes and let herself tune in to the low rumble of his voice. 'Like what?'

Was that a resigned sigh through the door?

'My family weren't all that well off, but we didn't starve. We were okay.'

Uh-huh…?

'But it was the nineties. The decade of excess and success, and all that.'

Eve lay her head against the back of the bath and just listened.

'I have a brother, too, Eve,' Marshall went on. 'And poverty wasn't really his thing. So he took matters into his own hands and got quite...creative. Before long, the whole neighbourhood knew he was the go-to for whatever soft-core drug they needed.'

She opened her eyes and stared at the bathroom ceiling. After a moment she murmured, 'Your brother was a dealer?'

'An entrepreneur, according to him.'

Right. 'How long did that last?'

'Until very recently I couldn't have answered that at all. But let's just say business is as good as ever for Rick. I don't really see him any more.'

No wonder Marshall could empathise about Travis. He knew exactly what it was like to lose a brother.

'Whose decision was that?'

The only sound in the long, long silence that followed was the dripping of the shower into the spa.

'It's complicated,' he finally said.

Yeah, wasn't it always?

'I struggled growing up with Rick for a brother.'

'Because he was a criminal?'

'Because he was a hero.' He snorted. 'This was the back suburbs, remember. Pretty rough area to grow up. People loved him, they loved what he sold and they scrambled to be part of his inner circle. And sometimes that meant scrambling over me.'

There was something so…suppressed in his voice.

Eve lifted her head. 'Are you talking about girls?'

'Girls. Friends. Even a teacher or two with insalubrious habits.'

Oh, poor teenage Marshall. 'You resented him.'

'No, I loved him.'

'But you hated that,' she guessed.

'It meant I was no different to them. The sycophants. I just wanted to despise him and be done with it.'

So, there were many ways to lose a brother, then.

'Do you miss him?' she whispered.

'I did. For a long while. It felt like he was all I had, growing up. But I just focused my attention on my work and suddenly a decade had passed and I hadn't really thought about him at all. Or my mother. Or Christine. Or what they were all doing together.'

She pushed herself up a little more. 'Christine is with your brother?'

'She was.'

The door rattled slightly again, but not the knob. Down lower. And that was when Eve realised how very close they were sitting to each other. Him sunk down onto the floor of the suite, leaning on the door. Her lying back in warm luxury.

And only a single thin wall between them.

No wonder Marshall was wary of people. And no wonder the tight pain in his voice. 'I'm sorry. I should have asked you about something else.'

'It's okay. I got myself out. It's history now.'

'How do you go from a bad neighbourhood to working for the Federal Government?'

He laughed and she realised how attached she'd become to that sexy little chuckle.

'It will shock you to learn that meteorology is not the sexiest of the sciences.'

Not sexy? Had any of them *seen* Marshall Sullivan?

'But that meant there were scholarships going wasting, and one of them came to me. And it came with on-campus residency.'

'The scholarship was your ticket out?'

'At first, but soon I came to love meteorology. It's predictive. Stats and signs and forecasting. You always know what's coming with weather.'

'No surprises?' she murmured.

'I guess I was just looking for a life where you could spot the truth of something before it found you.'

Yeah. Given he'd been used by his earlier friends, cast off by his mother and then betrayed by his brother, maybe that wasn't surprising.

'It suits you.'

'Being a weatherman?'

'Busting the stereotype.' And how. 'I'm sorry I called you Weatherman.'

'I don't mind it as a nickname. As long as it's coming from you.'

'Why?' She laughed. 'What makes me so special?'

His answer, when it came, was immediate. 'How long have you got?'

The same kind of warmth that was soaking into her from without started to spread out from within. But she wrestled it back down. She couldn't afford to be feeling warm and fuzzy about anyone right now.

She made much of sitting up straighter in the spa bath. The bathroom equivalent of shuffling papers. 'Speaking of specials…what's on the menu tonight?'

Subtle, Read, real subtle.

But he let it go after a breath-stealing moment of indecision. 'Give me a second, I'll check.'

Good man, knows what he wants and compassionate.

Marshall Sullivan was just getting harder and harder to not like.

CHAPTER NINE

THIS WASN'T GOING to end well for him…

It had dawned on Marshall, somewhere between sitting at the bathroom door with his head tipped back against the timber and watching Eve tuck so enthusiastically into a bowl of Italian soup, that not everyone was rewarded for goodness. Any more than they were rewarded for doing the right thing.

Hadn't he got that by now?

But done was done. He'd made his choice and he was here. Only time would tell whether it was a crazily fatalistic or brilliantly optimistic decision. But since he was here and since she hadn't driven him off the road, he could use the time practically. He could try and get to know Eve a bit more. Understand her.

Maybe that way he could get a sense of her truth before it hit him like a cyclone.

'Can I ask you what happened with Travis?' he asked, passing his empty plate into the long fingers she reached out and starting at the most obvious point. 'When he disappeared.'

Her bright, just-fed eyes dulled just a little.

'One day he was there—' she shrugged '—the next he was gone.'

'That simple?'

'It wasn't simple.'

'Losing someone never is.'

He fell to silence and waited her out. It had certainly worked well enough on him while she was in the bath. He'd offered up much more than he'd ever shared with anyone else.

'She was drunk,' Eve finally murmured and he didn't need to ask who. 'She'd passed the few hours of Travis's Under-Fifteens hockey at the nearest pub. As far as anyone could tell, she thought she was okay to drive.'

Oh. Crap. Drunk and in charge of the safety of a fourteen-year-old boy.

'Was she an alcoholic?' That certainly explained Eve's moderate approach to liquor.

Her dark head slowly nodded. 'And the whole neighbourhood got to hear about it.'

He let his hands fall between his splayed thighs. Stared at them. 'That's a lot for a girl to handle.'

'It was a lot for all of us to handle,' she defended.

'Travis watched Mum die, Dad endured her reputation being trashed and I...'

'What did you do?'

'I coped. I got on with things. Took over caring for them both.'

'A lot of pressure.'

'Actually, it was okay then.' *Then...* 'It gave me something to focus on. Purpose.

'Dad pulled Trav out of school for the last few months of the year and that might have been a mistake. It took him from his friends, his sport, his structure. He lost his way a bit. He got back into it the next year and got okay grades but he was never cheeky and joyous again. I think we all just got used to the new, flat Travis.' She took a big swallow of water. 'Maybe we got used to a new *us*, too.'

Yeah. Numbness crept up on a person...

'It wasn't easy, those first couple of years. At first it was all about getting him out of the hospital, but then life had to... We had to just get on with it, you know?'

Yep. He certainly did know all about just getting on... Story of his life. But not everyone could do it. There were times *he* really wanted to just opt out. In some ways maybe he had.

'What changed? To make him leave?'

Her beautiful face pinched up slightly. 'Um...'

Whatever it was, it was hurting her.

'There was an inquest the year he went, and there was all this media interest in the accident again.'

'Years later?'

'A legal queue, I guess.' Her slight shoulders shrugged and he'd never wanted to hold someone more in his life. But she looked so fragile he worried she'd shatter. 'So much pressure on all of us again.'

He shifted closer. Leaned into her. 'He couldn't take it?'

Her head came up but she didn't quite meet his eyes. 'I couldn't. I desperately wanted to understand what happened but I couldn't go through it all again. Supporting Dad, mothering Travis. Just as things were getting normal. I just couldn't do it while we relived the accident over and over again.'

Suddenly her blazing need to find her brother began to make more sense.

'What did you do?'

'I went back to my own place. Replaced the dead pot plants with new ones, cleaned the gutters, threw out years of junk mail, started easing back into my own life.'

'And what did Travis do?'

'I didn't abandon them,' she defended hotly. 'I still visited, did sisterly things. But they were both men. They needed to step up, too. They agreed.'

He said nothing, knowing the question was almost certainly in his eyes. *But...?*

'Trav was finding it harder than any of us realised. The inquest brought it all back just as he might have started to become stronger. He turned eighteen, and drifted further and further from us emotionally.' She shook her head. 'And then he just left. Right in the middle of the inquest. We thought he'd just taken off for a few days to avoid the pressure but then it was a week, and then two. We finally reported him missing when we hadn't heard anything for a month.'

'You blame yourself.'

Her slim shoulders lifted and then sagged again. 'I wasn't there for him.'

'Yeah, you were. For years.'

'But I withdrew.'

'You *survived*. Big difference.'

Her tortured eyes lifted. 'Why wouldn't he talk to me? If he was struggling.'

Yeah—she'd been carrying that around a while; he recognised the signs of soul baggage.

'Eighteen-year-old boys don't talk to anyone about their feelings, Eve. I've been that kid.'

Old agony changed her face. He pulled her into his arms. 'You aren't responsible for Travis being missing.'

'That's what people say, isn't it,' she said against

his chest. 'In this kind of situation. But what if I am?'

Okay, so she'd heard this before and still not believed it. A rough kind of urgency came over him.

'What if it had nothing to do with you and everything to do with a young boy who watched his mother die? On top of the day-to-day trauma of having an alcoholic for a mother. My own mother was no prize,' he admitted, 'but she was at least present.'

He'd almost forgotten that she was Eve's mother, too. She seemed so disconnected from her past. 'What if you had turned up on his doorstep every single day and he had still done this?'

Tortured eyes glistened over. 'He's my brother.'

'He's a grown man, Eve.'

'Only just. Eighteen is still a kid. And with the anxiety disorder, and depression…'

'Which he was being treated for, right? He was on it.'

'Then why did he leave?'

It was always going to come back to that question, wasn't it? And Eve was never going to be free of the big, looming question mark. 'Only Travis knows.'

She fell to an anguished kind of silence, picking at the fabric on the sofa beneath her. Marshall stacked up the rest of the dishes and put the lot outside his door on the tray left there by the staff and quietly turned back. He crossed to her and held out a hand.

'Come on.'

She peered up at him with wide, hurt eyes. 'Where are we going?'

'I'm walking you home. I think you need to be in your own place right now, surrounded by familiar things.'

She didn't argue for once. Instead, she slipped her fingers into his and let him pull her up and towards the suite's door.

'It's not really my place,' she murmured as they stepped out into the hall. 'And most of them aren't my things.'

How weird that such sorrowful words could bring him such a lurch of hope. If Eve wasn't all that attached to the Bedford or its contents maybe there was hope for him yet. Maybe he could wedge himself a place in her distracted, driven world.

He kicked off one of his shoes and left it wedged in the doorway so that he didn't lock himself out.

Down in the almost empty car park he opened the bus for her and followed her through to her bedroom. She didn't so much as glance at that presumption, and she didn't look the slightest bit anxious that he might stay. She just accepted it as though they'd been doing it for years.

He pressed his key-card into her hand. 'Breakfast on the balcony at eight?'

'Okay.'

He flipped back her bed covers and waited for her to crawl in, then he folded them back over her and tucked her so firmly in that she resembled something that had just tumbled out of a sarcophagus.

'It's not your fault, Eve.'

He was going to tell her that every day of their lives if he had to.

She nodded, but he wasn't foolish enough to think that she actually believed it. Maybe she just accepted that he didn't think so. Bending brought him dangerously close to her lips, but he veered up at the last moment and pressed his to her hot forehead instead.

'Breakfast. Eight o'clock.'

She didn't agree. She didn't even nod. But her eyes were filled with silent promise and so he killed the lights and backed out of the room and then the bus, giving the big back door a security rattle before leaving her snug and safe inside.

It went against everything in him to leave her in the car park, but Eve had been doing this a long time

and she was a grown, competent woman. Just because she'd opened up a little and shown him some
of her childhood vulnerability didn't mean he could
treat her like the child she'd almost been when her
mother killed herself and nearly her brother.

As hard as that was.

He limped along on one shoe and returned to the
big, lonely suite.

A gentle kind of rocking roused Marshall out of a
deep, comfortable sleep. The suite was as dark as
an outback road but he knew, instantly, what was
going on.

Except it wasn't eight o'clock. And this wasn't
morning.

A warm, soft body slid in next to him, breathing
carefully. He shunted over a bit to make room, but
she only followed him, keeping their bodies close.

'Eve…?'

As if there was any question.

She snuggled up hard into his side. 'Shh. It's late.'

Or early, he suspected. But he wasn't about to
argue with whatever God had sent her back to him,
and he wasn't about to ruin a good thing by reading
something into this. Instead, he took it—and Eve—
at face value and just gathered her into him so that
his sleepy heat could soak into her cold limbs.

But he wasn't so strong that he could resist pressing his lips to her hair and leaving them there.

And she wasn't of a mind to move away, apparently.

'I have no expectations,' he murmured against her scalp. 'If you tell me that going our separate ways yesterday felt okay to you then that's cool, I know where I stand. But it felt anything but okay to me and I came back so that we could just—'

'Finish things up more civilly?'

'—*not* finish things up,' he said into the dark. 'Maybe just explore this a little more. See where it goes.'

Her breathing filled his ears. His heart.

'I slept with you because you were riding off into the horizon the next day,' she whispered.

He turned a little more towards her, trying to make her out in the dark. 'And I slept with you knowing that. But then I discovered something about horizons.'

'What?' she mumbled.

'They're an awfully long way away.'

She pushed up onto one elbow, robbing him of her warmth. 'So…you're just going to ride shotgun for the next…what—days? Weeks?'

'Until we know.'

Her voice sounded tantalisingly close to his ear. 'Know what?'

'Whether we have potential.'

'You're in the middle of an epic road trip. It's a terrible time to be looking for potential.'

She was right. He should be aiming for fast, casual and uncomplicated. Like she had.

'That's the thing, Eve. I wasn't looking. It seems to have found me.'

She had nothing to say to that, but her steady breathing told him she was still awake.

Listening.

Thinking.

He bundled her back in close and fell with her—lips to hairline—into a deep slumberous heaven.

CHAPTER TEN

WAKING THE NEXT morning was like an action replay of the morning before—but without all the action. This time, he didn't catch Eve creeping out of bed. This time, she was not freaking out and sucking all the warmth out of the room. This time, she was not back-pedalling madly from what they'd shared the night before.

Even though what they'd shared overnight was more intimate and meaningful than anything they'd done with each other back at the campsite.

Two bodies, pressed together in sleep. Wrapped around each other. Talking.

No sex.

But infinitely more loaded.

'Morning,' she murmured before her eyes even opened.

'How long have you been awake?'

'Long enough to feel you staring.'

'It's the novelty.' He chuckled.

Come on. Open them...

But she just smiled and squirrelled in closer, as if she was getting ready to go back to sleep.

'It's eight o'clock,' he pointed out.

And then her eyes opened—drugged, languorous, and he'd never seen anything quite so beautiful.

'No, it's not.'

'Yeah, it really is.'

And this was a workday for both of them. Technically.

Her eyes fluttered shut and she wiggled deeper into the covers. Okay, so he was going to have to be the brave one.

'So, look at you in my bed...' he hinted.

One eye half opened and he waited for the quip to follow. Something sharp and brilliant and completely protective. But he didn't get one. Her second eye opened and locked on him, clear and steady.

'I just woke up in the middle of the night,' she murmured, 'and knew this is where I wanted to be.'

Right. What could he say to that? This was what he'd come back for, wasn't it? To see what might grow between them. Wasn't that what he'd been murmuring at midnight about? Yet, now that he was faced with it, it suddenly seemed overwhelmingly real.

He cleared his throat. 'Breakfast?'

'In town, maybe? After I get set up.'

Right. Work.

'I have to do my thing today, too.' For the people paying him.

'Where's the weather station?'

He told her and she asked a question or two. More than enough to muddle his mind. He was in bed with a living, breathing, *radiating* woman and they were talking about the weather again. Literally. But somehow it didn't feel like small talk. It felt big.

And then it hit him why.

They were having a *couple* conversation. Comfortable. Easy. And they were having it in bed. Where all conversations should happen. And that was enough to scare him upright.

'I'm going to grab a shower, then I'll get us some food while you set up.'

She pushed up onto her elbows, blinking. 'Sorry if I made things weird.'

He forced a relaxed smile onto his face.

'Not weird. Just—' *dangerously appealing* '—new.'

He padded into the bathroom and put himself under the shower Eve had enjoyed so much the night before. Images filled his head—of Eve standing with the water streaming over her slight body, head tipped back, issuing those sounds he'd heard while he leaned on the doorframe out in the hall. How badly he'd wanted to step inside and join her. Shower with her until the end of time. And now, here he was freaking out that his dreams might be coming true.

In his world, dreams didn't come true.

They shattered.

It was so hard to trust the good feelings.

He nudged the taps and cut out half of the hot water feed and then made sure to keep his shave brief.

When he emerged, Eve was gone.

For half a heartbeat the old doubts lurched to the surface but then he remembered she had no clothes up here, only what she'd crept up the stairs in, and he opened the suite door a crack and peered down through the hallway window. Like a seasoned stalker. Long enough to see Eve heading back across the car park.

Come on, man. Pull it together. This is what you wanted.

He'd just learned the hard way not to want. It only led to disappointment.

So Eve had opted for more comfortable accommodation overnight. No biggie. That was hardly a declaration of passion. She'd snuggled in and enjoyed the heat coming off him, and today she was all about Travis again.

Eve was always about Travis.

It was part of what intrigued him about her. That fathomless compassion.

But it was part of what scared him, too. Because how could there be room for him with all that emotion already going on?

He quickly shrugged something decent on and ran a quick comb through his hair so that when she swiped the suite's door he was clothed and everything that needed brushing was brushed.

He threw her a neutral smile. 'Good to go?'

The pause before she answered was full of silent query. 'Yep. Meet you in front of the Town Hall?'

Wherever that was. 'Yup.'

The question mark shifted from her eyes to her soft smile but she simply turned and let him follow her back down to where his bike was parked. She headed for the bus.

'Egg and bacon burger?' he called.

'Sounds great.'

Great.

Okay, so it was officially his turn to be off. Most guys would be stoked to wake up to a warm, willing body but, instead of converting the opportunity to a goal, he'd let it get under his skin. Weird him out. Not the best start, true, but Eve didn't look too tragic about it. Her mind was back on her brother already.

As was always the way.

* * *

The bumbling MP yesterday was pretty normal, in Eve's experience. In fact, he'd been more tactful than many of the people she'd tried to explain herself to in the past.

Herself… Her choices.

But the only people who'd understood her odyssey the way Marshall had were the other family members in her missing-persons network. Which did, in fact, make him pretty darned exceptional.

Eve smiled and passed a poster to an older lady who stopped to peruse her display. The stranger took her time and looked at every single face before wandering off, which Eve particularly appreciated. Nothing worse than the glancers. Glancing was worse than not looking at all, in some ways. Eve knew it was a big ask to hope that people might remember one face, let alone dozens, but there was no chance of people remembering them from the wall displays in post offices that were half obscured by piles of post packs or pull-down passport photo screens most of the time.

Something inside her had shifted last night when Marshall told her about his brother. As if he went from adversary to equal in her mind. He'd effectively lost a brother, too—to circumstance—so he knew what it was like to give up on a family member.

Except, in Marshall's case, he was the one who'd walked away.

And didn't that tear her up. Half of her wanted to hug him for the personal strength it must have taken to leave an intolerable family situation so young. The other half wanted to shake him and remind him he had a brother. A living, breathing brother.

And those weren't to be sneezed at.

She never would have picked him for the product of a rough neighbourhood, even with all the tattoos. He was just too *normal*. Beneath the 'keep your distance' leather smokescreen. But to find out that someone so close to him was neck-deep in criminal activity… That just made what he'd done with his life even more remarkable. Finished school, tackled university and then got himself the straightest and smartest of straight, smart jobs.

Meteorology.

A tiny smile crept, unbidden, to her lips. Who knew that she'd ever get quite so hot and bothered by a weatherman?

Yet here she was, very much bothered. And decidedly hot under the covers.

At least she had been last night.

Crawling in with him hadn't been quite the spontaneous exercise she'd confessed. The sprint across the car park had been as sobering as it was chilly and she had plenty of opportunity to think better of it. But she hadn't—because a big part of her had wanted him to roll over, see her and just keep on rolling. Up and over onto her. To make love to her like he had the first time—all breathless and uninhibited.

Another taste of lightness.

Her days were consumed by her brother—couldn't someone else have her nights? When she'd normally be asleep? Wouldn't it be okay to let go just for those few short hours? To forget?

But Marshall hadn't taken advantage. He'd just tugged her close, murmured hot, lovely words in her ear and pulled her into unconsciousness behind him. And it was only as she'd fallen asleep that she'd realised how badly she wanted *not to* do the obvious thing. The easy thing.

Sleeping with Marshall was easy.

Falling for him would be treacherous.

But morning would always come. And it dragged reality with it.

Eve's reality was that she still had a monumental task ahead of her. Marshall had chased her up the highway to see what might form between them if they gave it a chance, but how could there be any kind of something between them while she had this dismal marathon to complete?

Good sex was one thing. A *happy families* future was quite another.

She had no room for anything beyond right now.

And both of them knew that *happy families* was just a myth. They knew it firsthand.

'Thank you,' she murmured belatedly to the man who took a poster as though from an unattended pile. She'd been so lost in thought, that might as well have been true.

Nope, she hadn't promised Marshall anything more than *right now* and he hadn't asked for it.

Two people could go a long way on *right now.*

The south-western corner of Western Australia was packed with small, wine-rich country towns, each with unique personality and spaced close enough for tourists to hop from one to another on their week-end trails.

Papering the two hundred square kilometres ahead with posters was going to be a much bigger job than the two thousand before it.

But they did a good job together, she and Marshall. When he wasn't working, or they weren't curled up together in her bus or a motel room, he'd be with her, plastering Trav's face all over the towns they visited. Handing her the pins or the tape or the staple gun. Nothing she couldn't have done for herself but—boy—was it good not to have to.

Somehow, having someone to share all of this with made it more bearable. And she hadn't realised how unbearable it had become. How utterly soul-destroying. Until she felt her soul starting to scab over.

She glanced sideways at Marshall's handsome face. How fast she'd adapted to having him here by her side during her displays of *The Missing*. How willing she'd been to bring him into her journey.

A problem shared…

A man approached from the far end of the street, folded paper in his hands. He looked grim and twitchy.

'Movie tonight?'

Marshall's voice pulled her focus back to him. The two of them hadn't braved a movie since *that* night in her bus. As if the entire art form was now too loaded. The last time they'd settled in to watch a movie together they'd ended up sharing so much more.

'Maybe,' she said breathlessly. A girl couldn't live on spooning alone. And she was fairly sure neither could a man. They were well overdue for a rematch.

The way Marshall's eyes locked on hers said maybe he thought so, too.

The stranger still hovered and it was only as he turned away, stuffing the paper in his pocket, that Eve's brain finally comprehended that he wanted to say something.

'I'm sorry,' she called, stretching taller in her seat. 'Can I help you?'

The man slowed. Turned.

'Do you know him?' he said, holding up the crumpled paper as he approached. It was one of her posters.

A tingle tickled between her shoulders and grew outwards until gooseflesh puckered under her shirt. 'He's my brother. Why? Do you recognise him?'

The man stepped one pace closer. 'Not sure. He looks familiar.'

Eve shot to her feet. 'What do you mean?'

'Just that I feel like I've seen him before. But I don't want to get your hopes up if I'm wrong...'

'I don't need certainty,' she was quick to reassure, 'just leads.'

She felt Marshall's heat as he stood behind her and her heart began to hammer. God, she'd been so wrapped up in the promise in his eyes she'd nearly let this guy walk off. A guy who might know something.

'Where do you think you know him from?' Marshall asked.

The guy switched focus. 'I really can't say. Just… somewhere. And recently.'

'How recent? Two months? Six?' Eve could hear the urgency in her own voice but was incapable of easing it. A big hand fell on her shoulder as if to physically suppress her.

'Where do you live?' Marshall asked, much more casually.

The guy responded to his even tone. 'Here. In Augusta. But I don't think I know him from here.'

God, the idea of that. That Travis might be right here in this little seaside town…

'Somewhere else?'

'I run trucks. Maybe I saw him on one of those. In another—'

'What other town?' Eve pressed, and Marshall squeezed harder.

Are you freaking kidding me? The first reasonable lead she'd had in nearly nine months and Marshall wanted her to relax? Every nerve in her body was firing in a soup of adrenaline.

'Where do you do your runs?' Marshall asked calmly.

'Anywhere in the South West,' the man said, visibly uncomfortable at having started the conversation at all. He immediately started retreating from his earlier thoughts. 'Look, I'm probably wrong—'

Deep panic fisted in her gut.

'*No!* Please don't start second-guessing yourself,' Eve rushed on, critically aware that her urgency was pushing him further away. She fought to breathe more evenly. God, how close she'd come to just not calling out to him.

What was happening to her?

'The subconscious is a powerful thing,' she urged. 'It probably knows something your conscious mind can't quite grasp.'

The man's eyes filled with pity and, in that moment, she saw herself as others must. As Marshall must.

Obsessed. Desperate. Pathetic.

And she didn't like his view of her one little bit.

Lines appeared on the man's time-weathered brow. 'I'm just not sure…'

'How about just jotting down the routes you usually take?' Marshall grabbed another poster, flipped it over to the blank side and handed it and a pen to the man. 'We can take it from there.'

More lines formed in his weathered skin. 'I have two-dozen routes. That'll take time…'

They were losing him. And the best lead she'd had in an age…

Eve dashed to the front of the bus and rummaged in the glove box with clammy hands for the maps she carried detailing every region she was in. One was marked up with her own routes—to make sure she never missed a town or junction—but her spare was blank, a clean slate. She thrust the spare into the man's hands.

'On this then, just highlight the routes you take. I can do the rest.'

Possibility flickered over his face. 'Can I take this with me?'

The fist squeezed harder. Not because she risked losing a four-dollar map. But she risked losing a tangible link with Travis. 'Can't you do it here…?'

'Take it,' Marshall interrupted. 'Anything you can give us will be great.'

The stranger's eyes flicked between the two of them 'Hopefully, I can be clearer somewhere…away from here.'

Eve took two steps towards the man as he retreated with the map in his hand. She spun to Marshall. 'I should go with him.'

His strong hand clamped around her wrist. 'No. You should let him go somewhere quiet and do what he has to do. He's not going to be able to concentrate with you hovering over him.'

Hovering…! As if they were talking about her

chaperoning a teenage date and not possibly finding her brother. 'I just want to—'

'I know exactly what you want, Eve, and how you're feeling right now. But stalking the guy won't get you what you need. Just leave him be. He'll come back.'

'But he's the first person that's seen Travis.'

'*Possibly* seen Travis, and if you push any harder he's going to decide he never actually saw a thing. Leave him to his process, Eve.'

She glanced up the street, hunting for the man's distinctive walk. Two blocks away she spotted him, turning into the local pub. She swung baleful eyes onto Marshall.

'Leave him to his process,' he articulated.

Deep inside she knew he was right, but everything in her screamed for action. Something. Anything.

'Easy for you to say!'

He took a long breath. 'There's nothing easy about watching you suffer, Eve.'

'Try feeling it some time,' she muttered.

She turned away roughly but he caught her. 'I do feel it. In you. Every day—'

'No, I mean try *feeling* it, Marshall. From this side of the fence.'

'It's not about sides—'

'Spoken like someone who's more used to cutting people out of their life than being cut out.'

For a moment she thought he was going to let that go, but he was a man, not a saint. Words blew warmly behind her ear as Marshall murmured in this public place, 'And what's that supposed to mean, exactly?'

'What you imagine it means, I'm sure,' she gritted.

'Eve, I know this is frustrating—'

She spun on him. 'Do you, Marshall? You've been travelling with me all of ten days. Multiply that by twenty-five and then tell me how you think I should be feeling as my only lead walks away from me and into a bar.'

His lips tightened but he took several controlled breaths. 'You need an outlet and I'm convenient.'

Spare me the psychoanalysis!

'How did this become about you?' she hissed. 'This is about me and Travis.'

She glanced at the pub again and twisted her hands together.

Warm fingers brought her chin around until her eyes met his. '*Everything* is about Travis with you, Eve. Everything.'

That truly seemed to pain him.

The judgment in his gaze certainly hurt her. 'Forgive me for trying to stay focused on my entire purpose out here.'

The words sounded awful coming off her lips, doubly so because, deep down, she knew he didn't deserve her cruelty. But did he truly not get the importance of this moment? How rare it was. How it felt to go nearly nine months without a single lead and then to finally get one?

A lead she'd almost missed because she was so off mission.

She dropped back into her seat.

All week she'd been going through the motions. Putting up posters, staffing her unhappy little table, answering questions about the faces in her display. But she hadn't actively promoted. She hadn't forced posters on anyone. She hadn't made a single real impression.

All she'd done was sit here looking at Marshall. Or thinking about him when he was gone. Letting herself buy into his hopeless fantasy.

She'd failed Travis. Again.

And she'd nearly missed her only lead.

Marshall sat back and considered her in silence. And when he spoke it was careful but firm.

'I think it might be time to stop, Eve.'

She did stop. All movement, all breath. And just stared.

'Maybe it's time to go home,' he continued. 'This isn't good for you.'

When she finally spoke it was with icy precision.

'How good for me do you imagine it is sitting around the house, wondering whether Travis is alive or dead and whether anyone will give him more than the occasional cursory check twice a year?'

'It's been a year—'

'I know. I've been living it every single day. But I'm nearly done.'

'You're not nearly done. You still have one third of the country to go.'

'But only ten per cent of the population,' she gritted.

'That's assuming that you haven't missed him already.' *And assuming he is still alive.* The words practically trembled on those perfect lips.

She glared. 'What happened to "What you're doing is logical"?'

'I meant that. I completely understand why you're doing it.'

'And so…?'

'I don't like what *it's doing to you*, Eve. This search is hurting you. I hate watching it.'

'Then leave. No one's forcing you to stay.'

'It's not that easy—'

But whatever logical, persuasive thing he was

about to say choked as she ran over the top of him. 'Maybe you're just unhappy that I'm putting him ahead of you. Maybe your male ego can't handle taking second place.'

She'd never seen someone's eyes bruise before, but Marshall's did. And it dulled them irreparably.

'Actually, that's the one thing I'm more than used to.'

The fist inside tightened further. How could she do this? How could she choose between two men she cared so much about? Marshall was, at least, stable and healthy and capable of looking after himself. Travis was...

Well, who knew what Travis was? Or where.

But his need was unquestionably greater.

She ripped the emotional plaster off and pushed to her feet. 'I think it's time for us to go our separate ways.'

The bruising intensified. 'Do you?'

'It's been lovely—'

'But you're done now?'

'Come on, Marshall, how long would we have been able to keep this up, anyway? Your circuit's coming to an end.' And her funds were running out.

Her casual dismissal turned the vacuum behind his lids to permafrost. 'Is that right?'

'I don't have room for you, Marshall.'

'No, you really don't, do you.'

'I need to stay focused on Travis.'

'Why?'

'Because he needs me. Who else is going to look for him?' Or look *out* for him. Like she should have all along.

'Face facts, Eve,' he said, face gentle but words brutal. 'He's either gone or he's *choosing* to stay away. You said it yourself.'

Her breaths seemed to have no impact on the oxygen levels in her body. Dark spots began to populate the edges of her vision. 'I can't believe that.'

'People walk away all the time. For all kinds of reasons.'

'Maybe *you* do.'

His voice grew as cold as her fingers. 'Excuse me?'

She started to shake all over. 'I should have thought to seek your perspective before. I have an expert on cutting loose right here with me. You tell me why a perfectly healthy young man would just walk away from his family.'

Marshall's face almost contorted with the control he was trying to exert. 'You think I didn't struggle, leaving them?'

'As far as I can see, you crossed a line through

them and walked away and you seem no worse for wear. That's quite a talent.'

'Are you truly that self-absorbed,' he whispered, 'that you can't appreciate what that was like for me?'

'Yet you chose it.'

Where were these words coming from? Just pouring like toxic lava over her lips. Uncontrollable. Unstoppable.

Awful.

'Sometimes, Eve, all your choices are equally bad and you just have to make one.'

'Just go and don't look back?' she gritted. 'Who does that?'

Something flared in his eyes. Realisation. 'You're angry at Travis. For leaving.'

I'm furious *at Travis for leaving*, she screamed inside. But outwardly she simply said, 'My brother left against his will.'

How many police counsellors had she had that argument with? Or fights with her father.

'What if he didn't?' Marshall urged. 'What if he left because he couldn't imagine staying?'

Pfff... 'Someone's been reading up on the missing-persons websites.'

'Don't mock me, Eve. I wanted to understand you better—'

'Those people were desperate or scared or sick. The Travis I know wouldn't do that.'

'Maybe he wasn't your Travis, have you thought about that? Maybe he's not the kid brother you raised any more.'

The trembles were full-body shudders now.

Marshall stepped closer. Lowered his voice. 'Do you see how much of your life he's consumed, Eve? This obsessive search. It's ruining you.'

'If I don't do it, who will?' she croaked.

'But at what cost?'

'My time. My money. All mine to spend.'

He took her hand. 'And how much of life are you missing while you're out here spending it? I'm right here, Eve. Living. Breathing. But any part of you that might enjoy that is completely occupied by some-one who's—'

His teeth cracked shut.

Nausea practically washed over her. 'Go on. Say it.'

'Eve—'

'Say it! You think he's dead.'

'I fear he's a memory, one way or another. And I think that memory is stopping you from living your life just as much as when your mother died.'

'Says the man who hides out behind a face full of hair and leather armour to avoid facing his demons.'

Marshall took a long silent breath.

'This has become an unhealthy obsession for you, Eve. A great idea, practically, but devastating personally. You stripped yourself away from all your support structures. Your colleagues. Your friends. Your family. The people who could have kept you healthy and sane.'

'So we're back to me being crazy?'

'Eve, you're not—'

'You need to go, Marshall,' she urged. 'I can't do what I have to do with you here. That guy nearly walked off because I was off my game. I was busy mooning after you.'

'This is my fault?'

She wrapped her arms around her torso. 'I nearly let my only lead in a year walk off because I was distracted with you.'

'I guess I should at least be happy I'm a distraction.'

Misery soaked through her. 'You are much more than a distraction, but don't you get it? I don't have room for you—for us—in my life. In my heart.'

'You don't have room for happiness? Doesn't that tell you anything?'

'I don't get to be happy, Marshall,' she yelled, heedless of the passers-by. 'Not until Travis is back home where he belongs.'

Those dreadful words echoed out into the sea-side air.

'Do you hear yourself, Eve? You're punishing yourself for failing Travis.'

The muscles around her ribs began to squeeze. Hard. 'Thank you for your concern but I'm not your responsibility.'

'So, I just walk away from you, knowing that you're slowly self-destructing?'

'I will be fine.'

'You won't be fine. You'll search the rest of the country and what will you do when you get back to your start point and you've found no sign of him? Start again from the top?'

The thought of walking away from this search without her brother was unimaginable.

'I will always look for him,' she vowed.

And that wasn't fair on someone as vibrant as Marshall. Hadn't he been sidelined enough in his life? She shook her head slowly.

'Find someone else, Marshall. Please.'

Someone who could offer him what he needed. Someone who wouldn't hurt him. Someone who could prioritise him.

'I don't want someone else, Eve,' he breathed. 'I want you.'

Those three simple words stole the oxygen from

her cells. The words and the incredibly earnest glitter of Marshall's flecked grey eyes that watched her warily now.

Of all the times. Of all the places. Of all the men.

The seductive rush of just letting all of this go, curling herself into Marshall's arms and letting him look after her. Letting him carry half of all this weight. Of parking the bus for good somewhere and building a new life for herself with whatever she had left. With him. Of little grey-eyed kids running amuck in the sand dunes. Learning to fish. Hanging out with their dad.

But the kids of her imagination morphed, as she watched, into Travis when he was little. Scrabbling along the riverbank at the back of their house. Getting muddy. Just being a kid. A kid she loved so completely.

Eve took several long breaths. 'If you care for me as much as you say you do, then what I need should matter to you. And what I need is my brother. Home. Safe. That's all I've got room for.'

'And then what?'

She lifted her eyes to his.

'After that, Eve. What's the plan then? You going to move in with him to make sure he stays safe? Takes his medication? Stays healthy? How far does this responsibility you feel go?'

The truth…? Just as there was nothing but black after not finding Travis, there was nothing but an opaque, uncertain mist after bringing him home. She'd just never let herself think about either outcome in real terms. She'd just focused on the ten kilometres in front of her at all times.

And the ten kilometres in front of her now needed to be solo.

She twisted her fingers into his. 'You're a fantastic guy, Marshall. Find someone to be happy with.'

'I thought I was working on that.'

It was time for some hard truths. 'You're asking me to choose between a man I've loved my whole life and a man I've—'

She caught herself before the word fell across her lips, but only just.

—*known ten days.*

No matter how long it felt.

Or how like love.

'Would I like to be important to you?' he urged. 'Yes. Would I like, two years from now, to live together in a timber cottage and get to make love to you twice a day in a forest pool beside our timber cabin? Yes. I'm not going to lie. But this is the real world. And in the real world I'm not asking you to choose *me*, Eve. I'm begging you to choose *life*. You cannot keep doing this to yourself.'

She stepped a foot closer to him, close enough to feel his warmth. She slid her unsteady hand up the side of his face and curled her fingers gently around his jaw.

'It's a beautiful image, Marshall,' she said past the ball of hurt in her chest. 'But if I'm going to indulge fantasies, it has to be the one where that guy with the map comes back and it leads me to finding Travis.'

The life drained right out of his face and his eyes dropped, but when they came back up they were filled with something worse than hurt.

Resignation.

This was a man who was used to coming last.

'You deserve to be someone's priority, Marshall,' she whispered. 'I'm so sorry.'

His eyes glittered dangerously with unshed truth and he struggled visibly to master his breathing, and then his larynx.

Finally he spoke.

'I'm scared what will happen to you if I can't be there with you to hold you—to help you—when you find him, or when you don't,' he enunciated. 'Promise me you'll go home to your father and start your life over and pick up where you left off.'

'Marshall—'

'Promise me, Eve. And I'll go. I'll leave you in peace.'

Peace. The very idea of that was almost laughable. Not knowing the true nature of the world, as she did now. Blissfully ignorant Eve was long gone.

And so she looked Marshall in the eye.

And she lied.

CHAPTER ELEVEN

DID EVE HAVE any idea how bad she was at deceit?

Or maybe she just saved her best lies for the ones she told herself. There was no way on earth that this driven, strong woman was going to go back to suburbia after this was all over.

She was too far gone.

And, try as he might, she was not letting him into her life long enough for him to have any kind of influence on what happened from here. His job was to walk away. To respect her decision.

To do what his brain said was right and not what his heart screamed was so very wrong.

I'm choosing Travis.

His gut twisted in hard on itself. Wasn't that the story of his life? Had he really expected the very fabric of the universe to have changed overnight? Eve needed to finish this, even if she had no true idea of what that might mean.

He needed her to be whole.

He just hadn't understood he was part of the rending apart.

He rested his hand over Eve's on his cheek, squeezed gently and then tugged hers down and over.

'I hope you find him,' he murmured against the soft skin of her palm.

What a ridiculously lame thing to say.

But it was definitely better than begging her to change her mind. Or condemning her to search, half-crazed, forever.

He stepped back. And then back again. And the cold air between them made it easier to take a very necessary third step. Within a few more, he was turning and crossing the road without a backward glance.

Which was how he generally did things.

You crossed a line through them and walked away.

Did she truly believe that he could cauterise entire sections of his life without any ill effect? That he was that cold? His issues arose from caring too much, not too little. But maybe she was also right about it being a life skill, because experience was sure going to help him now.

This was every bit as hard as walking away from his mother and brother.

Eve was not going to be okay. He could feel it in

his bones. She had no idea how much she needed him. Someone. Anyone. And if he could feel that protective of her after just a few short weeks, how much must she burn with the need to find and protect the baby brother she'd loved all his life?

He kept walking up the main street through town but then turned down a side street as soon as he was out of her view and doubled back to slide in the side door of a café fronting onto the same road he'd just walked down. From his table he could see Eve, behind her display table, rocking back and forth in the cold air.

If that guy didn't come back soon, he was going to go and drag him out of that pub and frogmarch him back up the street. If Eve wasn't going to walk away from this whole crusade, and she wasn't going to have him by her side, then he was going to do everything he could to make sure that it all came out okay.

So that *she* came out okay.

The waitress delivered his coffee and he cupped his frigid hands around it and watched the woman who'd taken up residence in the heart he'd assumed was empty. The organ he thought had long since atrophied from lack of use.

She sat, hunched, surrounded by *The Missing*, curled forwards and eyes downcast. Crying in body if not in tears. Looking for all the world as bereft and miserable as he felt.

She wasn't trying to hurt him. She hadn't turned into a monster overnight. She was just overwhelmed with the pressure of this unachievable task she'd set herself.

She just had priorities. And he couldn't be one of them. It was that simple.

At least she'd been honest.

And if he was going to be, she'd never pretended it was otherwise. She'd never promised him more than right now. No matter what he'd hoped for.

So maybe he was making progress in life after all. At this rate he might be ready for a proper relationship by the time he was in his sixties.

Out on the street, Eve's body language changed. She pushed to her feet, as alert and rigid as the kangaroos they drove past regularly, her face turned towards the sea. A moment later, the guy from the pub shuffled back into view, handed her the folded map and spoke to her briefly, pointing a couple of times to places on the map.

Marshall's eyes ignored him, staying fixed on the small face he'd come to care so much about. Eve nodded, glanced at the map and said something brief before farewelling him. Then she sank back down onto her chair and pulled the map up against her chest, hard.

And then the tears flowed.

Every cell in his body wanted to dump his coffee and jog back across the road. To be there for her. To hold her. Impossible to know whether the guy had been unable to help, after all, and the tears were heartbreak. Or maybe they were joy at finally having a lead. Or maybe they were despair at a map criss-crossed with dozens of routes which really left her no further ahead than she'd started.

He'd never know.

And the not ever knowing might just kill him.

His fingers stilled with the coffee cup halfway to his mouth. At last, he had some small hint of what hell every day was for Eve. Of why she couldn't just walk away from this, no matter how bad it was becoming for her. Of why she had no room for anything—or anyone—else in her heart. Adding to the emotional weight she carried around every day was not going to change the situation. Loving her, no matter how much, was not going to transform her. There was only one thing that would.

Someone needed to dig that brother of hers out from under whatever rock he'd found for himself. For better or worse.

A sudden buzzing in his pocket startled him

enough to make him spill hot coffee over the edge of his mug and he scrambled to wipe the spillage with a napkin with one hand while fishing his phone out with the other.

He glanced at the screen and then swiped with suddenly nerveless fingers.

'Rick?'

'Hey,' his brother said. 'I've got something for you.'

Thank God for Rick's shady connections. And for health regulators. And maybe for Big Brother.

And thank God, for Eve's sake, that Travis Read was, apparently, still alive.

Rick had hammered home that the kid's name wouldn't have appeared anywhere on official records, if not for a quietly implemented piece of legislation at the start of the year. Even this was an *unofficial* record.

Accessing it certainly was—his brother had called in a number of very questionable favours getting something useful.

'The trouble with the Y-Gen is that they soon work out how to fly under the digital radar,' Rick had said over the phone. 'But he came undone by refilling his Alprazolam in his real name, even though he did it off the health scheme to stay hidden.

'As of February,' he'd continued, 'it became notifiable in order to reduce the amount of doc-shopping being done by addicts. Your guy wouldn't have known that because the GPs aren't required to advise their patients of its existence; in fact it's actively discouraged. And people call *me* dodgy...'

Marshall had ignored Rick's anti-government mutterings and scribbled the details down on the first thing at hand. The name of the drug. The town it was filled in. Ironic that prioritising his mental health had led to Travis's exposure. An obscure little register inside the Department of Health was pretty much the only official record in the entire country that had recent activity for Travis Read. Lucky for him, his brother knew someone who knew someone who knew some*thing* big about a guy in the Health Department's IT section. Something that guy was happy to have buried in return for a little casual database scrutiny.

Marshall's muttered thanks were beyond awkward. How did you thank someone for breaking innumerable laws on your behalf? Even if they did it every day.

'Whoever you're doing this for, Marsh...' Rick had said before hanging up '...I hope they know what this cost you. I sure do.'

That was the closest he'd come to acknowledging everything that went down between them in the past. He'd added just one more thing before disconnecting.

'Don't leave it so long next time.'

And then his brother was gone. After ten years. And Marshall had a few scribbled words on half a coffee-stained napkin. The pharmacy and town where Travis Read had shown his face a few months earlier.

Northam. A district centre five hours from where he was sitting.

Marshall pulled up his map app and stared at it. If Eve's intelligence was hereditary, then chances were her brother wouldn't be dumb enough to get his medical care in the town in which he was hiding out. So, he desktopped a wobbly fifty-kilometre radius around Northam and ruled out anything in the direction of the capital city. Way too public. It was also ninety-five per cent of the state's population and so that left him with only two-dozen country towns inside his circle.

If it was *him* trying to go underground, he'd find a town that was small enough to be under-resourced with government types, uninteresting enough to be off the tourist trail, but not so small that his arrival and settling in would draw attention. That meant tiny communities were out and so were any of the popular, pretty towns.

Agricultural towns were in because they'd be perfect for a man trying to find cash work off the books.

All of that filtering left him just a couple of strong candidates inside his circle. One was the state's earthquake capital and drew occasional media attention to itself that would be way too uncontrollable for a kid intent on hiding out.

That left only some towns on the southern boundary of his circle.

One was on a main route south—too much passing traffic and risk of exposure. Another too tiny.

The third was Beverley, the unofficial weekend headquarters for a biker gang and must regularly receive police attention.

He was about to cross that one through when he reconsidered. What better place to hide out than in a town filled with people with many more secrets to keep than Travis? People and activity that kept the tourists away and the authorities well and truly occupied. And where better for a newcomer to assimilate seamlessly than a town with a transient male population?

Beverley made it onto his top three. And he made a mental note to wear as much leather as he owned.

One day's drive away and he could spend a day each hunting in all three.

Then at least he would know.

It could be him.

Hard to say under the scrappy attempt at facial hair. The best of all the options he'd seen in the past couple of days, anyway. Marshall settled in at the bar and ordered something that he couldn't remember just five seconds later. Then he pulled out his phone and pretended to check his messages while covertly grabbing an image of the man that might be Eve's brother.

Evidence that Travis was alive and well.

If that even was him. Hard to tell from this far away.

There was an easy kind of camaraderie between the young man and his companions, as if an end-of-day beer was a very common thing amongst them. How nice that Travis got to sit here enjoying a beer with mates while his sister cried herself into an ulcer every night. Well-fed, reasonably groomed, clearly not here under any kind of duress, the kid seemed to have a pretty good gig going here in the small biker town.

Just before six, he pushed back from the table and

his mates let him go easily, as if skipping out early was business as usual.

Out on the footpath, Marshall followed at a careful distance. How much better would the photo be if he could give the authorities an address to go with the covertly captured picture?

Authorities.

Not Eve.

This was about giving her back her brother, not getting back into her good books. Something he could do to help. Instead of hurt.

He was no better for Eve than she was for him. He'd finally accepted that.

The guy turned down a quiet street and then turned again almost immediately. Marshall jogged to catch up. The back of these old heritage streets were rabbit warrens of open backyards and skinny laneways. A hundred places for someone to disappear into their house. The guy turned again and Marshall turned his jog into a sprint, but as he took the corner into the quiet laneway he pulled up short.

The guy stood, facing him, dirty steel caps parted, ready to run, arms braced, ready for anything.

In a heartbeat, he recognised how badly he might have blown this for Eve. How easy it would be for Travis to just disappear again, deeper into Australia, where she'd never ever find him. And he realised, on a lurch of his stomach, that this cunning plan was maybe going to come completely unstuck.

And it would have his name all over it.

'Who sent you?' the guy challenged, dark eyes blazing in the dusk light.

Marshall took a single step forward. 'Travis?'

'Who sent you?' he repeated, stepping back. As he moved and the light shifted slightly, the facet of those blazing eyes changed and looked to him more like fear and less like threat.

And he'd know those eyes anywhere…

Marshall lifted both hands, palms outward, to show he came in peace.

'I'm a friend of your sister.'

CHAPTER TWELVE

'HEY...'

Marshall's voice was startling enough out of the silence without her also being so horribly unprepared for it. Eve's stomach twisted back on itself and washed through with queasiness.

She'd only just resigned herself to him being gone—truly gone—and now he was back? What the hell was he trying to do—snap her last remaining tendrils of emotional strength?

She managed to force some words up her tight throat. 'What are you doing here, Marshall?'

It felt as if she was forever asking him that.

Compassion from him was nearly unbearable, but it rained down on her from those grey eyes she'd thought never to see again.

'Sit down, Eve.'

Instantly her muscles tensed. Muscles that had heard a lot of bad news. 'Why?'

'I need to talk to you.'

'About...?'

'Eve. Will you just sit down?'

No. No... He was looking at her like her father had the day Travis was officially declared a missing person.

'I don't think I want to.'

As if what she wanted would, in any way, delay what she feared was to come.

'Okay, we'll do this upright, then.'

His mouth opened to suck in a deep breath but then snapped shut again in surprise. 'I don't know where to start. Despite all the trial runs I've had in my mind on the way back here...'

That threw her. Was he back to make another petition for something between them? She moved to head that off before he could begin. Hurting him once had been bad enough...

'Marshall—'

'I have news.'

News. The tightness became a strangle in her throat. Somehow she knew he wouldn't use that word lightly.

'You're freaking me out, Marshall,' she squeezed out.

The words practically blurted themselves onto his lips. 'I've found Travis.'

The rush of blood vacating her face left her suddenly nauseous and her legs started to go.

'He's alive, Eve,' he rushed to add.

That extra piece of information knocked the final support from under her and her buckling legs deposited her onto the bus's sofa.

'Eve...' Marshall dropped down next to her and enveloped her frigid hand between both of his. 'He's okay. He's not hurt. Not sick.'

Eve's lips trembled open but nothing came out and it distantly occurred to her that she might be in shock. He rubbed her frigid fingers and scanned her face, so maybe he thought so, too.

'He's living and working in a small town here in Western Australia. He has a job. A roof over his head. He's okay.'

Okay. He kept saying that, but her muddled mind refused to process it. 'If he was okay he'd have been in touch...'

And then his meaning hit her. New job and new house meant new life. They meant *voluntary.* Her heart began to hammer against her ribs. Everything around her took on an other-worldly gleam and it was only then she realised how many tears wobbled right on the edges of her lashes.

'Where is he?' she whispered.

It was then Marshall's anger finally registered and confusion battled through the chaos in her mind.

Anger at her? Why? But colour was unquestionably high in his jaw and his eyes were stony.

'I can't tell you, Eve.'

Okay, her brain was seriously losing it. She waited for the actual meaning to sink in but all she was left with was his refusal to tell her where her long-lost brother was.

'But you found him…?'

'He asked me not to say.'

'What? No.' Disbelief stabbed low in her gut. And betrayal. And hurt. 'But I love him.'

'I know. *He* knows,' he hurried to add, though the anger on his face wasn't diminishing. 'He told me that he would disappear again if I exposed him. So that you'd never find him. He made me give him my word.'

Pain sliced across her midsection. 'But you don't even know him. You know mc.'

You love *me.*

She might as well have said it. They both knew it to be true. Not that it changed anything.

'Eve, he's alive and safe and living a life. He's on his meds and is getting healthy. Every day. He just can't do that at home.'

The thump against her eardrums intensified. 'Okay, he doesn't have to come back to Melbourne. We could move—'

'It's not about Melbourne, Eve. He doesn't want to go *home*.'

Realisation sunk in and she whispered through the devastation, 'He doesn't want to be with his family?'

God, did she look as young and fragile as her disbelief sounded? Maybe, because Marshall looked positively sick to be having this conversation.

'He wants to be healthy, Eve. And he needed to start over for that to happen.'

Start over...

'He doesn't have to come back, I can go to him. If he likes where he is—'

'I'm so sorry.' He squeezed both his hands around both of hers and held on. And, after an endless pause, he spoke, leaning forward to hold her stinging eyes with his. 'He doesn't want you to come, Eve. Particularly you.'

Particularly you.

Anguish stacked up on top of pain on top of misery. And all of it was wrapped in razor blades.

'But I love him.'

His skin blanched. 'I know. I'm so sorry.'

'I need to see him,' she whispered. 'I've been searching for so long—'

'He wants a fresh start.'

A fissure opened up in her heart and began to tug

wider. Her voice, when it came, was low and croaky. 'From me?'

'From everything.'

'Is this…' The fissure stretched painfully. 'Is this about *me*?'

Pity was like a cancer in his gaze. 'He can't be with you any more. Or your dad.'

'Why?' Her cry bounced off the Bedford's timber-lined walls.

Words seemed to fail him. He studied his feet for the barest of moments and then found her gaze again.

'Because of your mother, Eve.'

She stared at him, lost. Confused. But then something surfaced in the muddle of pain and thought. 'The accident?'

His expression confirmed it.

God, she could barely breathe, let alone carry on a conversation. 'But that was years ago.'

'Not for him, Eve. He carries it every day. The trauma. The anxiety. The depression. The guilt.'

Guilt? 'But Mum wasn't his fault.'

His fingers tightened around hers again and his gaze remained steady. 'It was, Eve. I'm so sorry.'

She shook the confusion away, annoyed to have to go back over such old ground. But being angry at him helped. It gave all the pain somewhere to go.

'No. He was with her, but... She was driving drunk.'

But she could read Marshall like a book—even after just a few weeks together—and his book said something else was going on here. Something big. She blinked. Repeatedly.

'Wasn't she?'

'Didn't you say they were both thrown from the bike?'

She was almost too dizzy for words. So she just nodded.

'And the police determined that she was in control?'

'Travis was the only other person there. And he couldn't ride properly then. He was underage.'

Marshall crouched over further and peered right into her face. Lending her his strength. 'No. He couldn't.'

But it was all starting to be horribly, horribly clear. *Oh, God...*

'Trav was driving?' she choked. Marshall just nodded. 'Because Mum had been drinking?'

No nod this time, just the pitying, horrible creasing of his eyes.

No... Not little Travis... 'And he never told anyone?'

'Imagine how terrified he must have been.'

A fourteen-year-old boy driving his drunk mother home to keep her safe and ending up killing her.

'He wouldn't have lied to protect himself.' Her certainty sounded fierce even to her.

'But what if he thought you'd all blame him? Hate him. That's a lot for someone to carry. Young or old. He can't face you.'

She sagged against the sofa back, this new pain having nowhere to go.

'He carried that all alone? All this time?' she whispered. 'Poor Trav. Poor baby...'

'No. Don't you take that on, too. He's getting treatment now. He's got support and he's getting stronger. He's doing pretty bloody well, all things considered.'

So why was Marshall still so very tense?

'But he knows what he wants. And needs. And he isn't going back to your world. And he doesn't want that world coming to him either.' He cursed silently. 'Ever.'

A tiny bit of heat bubbled up beneath her collar and she'd never been so grateful for anger. It cut like a hot knife through the butter of her numb disbelief and reminded her she could still feel something. And not a small something. The feelings she'd been suppressing for twelve months started to simmer and then boil up through the cracks of Marshall's revelation.

Ever.

'So…that's it?' she wheezed. 'I gave up a year of my life to find him—I broke my heart searching for him—and all this time he's been living comfortably across the country *starting over*?'

Marshall's lips pressed together. 'He's made his choice.'

'And you've made yours, apparently. You've taken his side pretty darned quick for a man you don't know.'

'Eve, I'm on your side—'

It was as if someone was puffing her with invisible bellows filled with hot air…making this worse and worse.

'Don't! How do I know you're not just making this all up to further your cause?'

'You can't be serious.'

'How would I know? The only evidence I have that any of this is true is your word. You might not have found him at all. You might just want me to think that. You might say anything to get me to stay with you.'

The words poured out uncontrollably.

'What the hell have I done to make you believe that of me?' But he rummaged in his pocket, pulled out his phone and opened his photo app. 'Believe this, then.'

Seeing Travis just about broke her heart.

Her baby brother. Alive. Healthy. Enjoying a beer. Even laughing. *Laughing!* She hadn't seen that in years.

She certainly hadn't done it in as long.

Tears tumbled.

'Eve—'

'What would happen, Marshall?' she asked desperately. 'If you told me where he is. How would he even know?'

She was flying through the stages of grief. At bargaining already.

'I know you, Eve...'

'So you're just going to take the choice away from me? Like some child?'

'You wouldn't be able to stay away. You know it.'

'I'm not about to *stalk him*, Marshall.'

'You already are, Eve! You're scouring the country systematically, hunting him down.'

Her gasp pinged around the little bus. 'Is that how you see it?'

'Why else would you want to know where he is? Unless you were going to keep tabs on him.'

'Because I *love* him. You have no right to keep this from me.'

'I'm not doing this to be a bastard, Eve. I don't want you in any more pain.'

'You think this doesn't hurt? Knowing he's alive and I can't get to him? Can't hold him? Or help him? You think that's kinder than letting me hear from his own lips that he doesn't want to come home?'

Just saying the words was horrible.

He took her chin in his fingers and forced her to look at him and, despite everything, her skin still thrilled at his simple touch. It had been days…

'Hear me, Eve,' he urged. 'If you go there he will disappear again. He knows what to do now, he'll be better at it and he might go off his meds to keep himself hidden. You will never see or hear from your brother again. Is that what you want?'

In all her wildest, worst dreams she'd never imagined she'd be sitting here, across from Marshall—of all people—fighting him for her brother's whereabouts.

But, dear Lord, fight she would.

'How is that any different to what I have now?'

'Because I know where he is and he's agreed to check in with me from time to time.'

The grief and hurt surged up right below her skin, preparing to boil over.

'So…what? You get to be some kind of gatekeeper to my family? Who the hell gave you that authority?'

'He has a legal right to go missing. He wasn't hurt,

or forced, or under any kind of duress. He decided to leave.'

'He was sick!'

'And managing his condition.'

He had an answer for every single argument. 'Then he must have been desperate.'

'Maybe, but he's not now. He's doing okay, I swear.' He caught her eyes again and brought everything back to the simple truth. 'You've found him, Eve.'

'No, *you* found him. I have as little as I had before.' Less, really. 'And, whatever he's going through, he clearly needs some kind of psychological help. People don't just walk out on perfectly good families.'

'They do, Eve. For all kinds of reasons. He couldn't stay, not knowing what he'd done. Fearing you'd discover it. Knowing how much you'd sacrificed—'

The inquest. The random timing of his disappearance suddenly came into crystal focus. 'I can help him.'

'You're still protecting him from responsibility? He's an adult, Eve. He doesn't want your help.'

'He needs it.'

'Does he, Eve? Or do you just need to believe that?'

She stiffened where she sat.

'You were his big sister. You looked after him and

your father after the accident. That became your role. And for the last twelve months you've been about nothing but him. You chucked in your job. You sold your house. What do you have if you don't have him?'

'I have…plenty, thanks very much. I'll go back to my career, reignite my friendships. Get a new place.'

Oh, such lies. There was no going back. She didn't even know how to be normal now.

'And then what? What are you if you're not all about your brother, Eve? You've been doing this since you were barely out of school.'

Furious heat sped up the back of her neck and she surged to her feet. 'Don't put this on me. You're choosing to protect him instead of me. How about we talk about that for a bit?'

He shot up right behind her and angry fists caught her upper arms. But he didn't shake her. It was more desperate and gentle than that.

'I would *never* protect him, Eve. I hate what he's done to you. I hate that I found him sitting in a pub having a relaxed beer with friends while your soul was haemorrhaging hope *every single day*. I hate that he's got himself a new life when he was gifted with *you* in his old one.'

He said 'you' as if that was something pretty

darned special. The stress faults in her heart strained that tiny bit more.

'I hate that he ditched you and your father rather than find the strength to work through it and that he didn't believe in your strength and integrity more.' He sucked in a breath. 'I would never put him ahead of you. I'm choosing *you*. This is all about you.'

'Then tell me where—'

'I can't!' he cried. 'He will disappear, Eve. The first sign of someone else looking for him. The first poster he sees in a neighbouring town. The first time his phone makes a weird noise. The next stranger who looks at him sideways in the street. He's dead serious about this,' he urged. 'Please. Just let it go.'

'How can I possibly do that?' she snarled.

'You once told me that all you wanted was to know he was all right. To have an answer. And nothing else mattered. Well, now you know. He's fine. But you're shifting the goalposts.'

'So, knowing is not enough! Maybe I do want him home, safe, with us. What's wrong with that?'

'Nothing. Except it's not achievable. And you need to accept that. It will be easier.'

'On who?'

'While your head and heart are full of your brother, then no one and nothing else can get through.'

'Are we back to that, Marshall? You and me?'

'No. You've been painfully clear on that front. I just wanted...'

He couldn't finish, so she finished for him. 'To save the day? To be the hero? Guess you weren't expecting to have to come back and be the bad guy, huh?'

'I didn't *have* to be anything.'

'You preferred to have me despise you?'

His eyes flared as if her words hit him like an axe. But he let her go and she stumbled at the sudden loss of his strength.

'You bang on about your great enduring love for your brother,' he grated. 'But you don't recognise it when it's staring you in the face. I chose *you* here today, Eve. Not myself and certainly not Travis. I am critically aware that the end of your suffering means the end of any chance for you and me. Yet here I am. Begging you to come back to the real world. Before it's too late.'

'Reality?' she whispered. 'Life doesn't get much realer than having someone you love ripped from you and held away, just out of reach.'

His eyes bled grey streaks. 'Finally. Something we agree on.'

He pushed away and walked to the bus's back door. But he caught himself there with a clenched fist on each side of the doorframe. His head sagged forward and his back arched.

Everything about his posture screamed pain.

Well, that made two of them.

But he didn't step forward. Instead, he turned back.

'You know what? Yes. Maybe I did want to be the man who took your pain away. Who ended all your suffering. Maybe I did want to see you look at me with something more heartfelt than curiosity or amusement or plain old lust.'

Haunted eyes bled.

'You're halfway to being missing yourself, emotionally speaking. And if Travis was found, then you'd have no choice but to return to the real, functional, living world. And I wanted to be the man that helped get you there.'

'Why?'

Frustrated hands flew up. 'Why do you think, Eve? Why do any of us do anything, ultimately?'

She blinked her stinging eyes, afraid to answer.

'*Love*, Eve.' So tired. So very weary. Almost a joke on himself. He made the word sound like a terminal condition. 'I love you. And I wanted to *give* you your heart's desire if I couldn't be it.'

'You barely know me,' she breathed.

'You're wrong.' He stepped up closer to her. Towered above her. 'You spend so much time stopping yourself from feeling emotion that you've forgotten to control how much of it you show. You're an open book, Eve.

'I know you're heartbroken about Travis betraying you like this,' he went on, 'and confused about loving him yet hating this thing he's done. I know you're desperate for somewhere to send all that pain, and you don't really want to throw it at me but you can't deal with it all yourself because you've closed down, emotionally, to cope with the past year. Maybe even longer. And it's easier to hate me than him.'

Tears sprang back into her eyes.

'I know it particularly hurts you that it's *me* that's withholding Travis from you because deep down you thought we had a connection even if you didn't have the heart to pursue it. You trusted me, and I've betrayed you. Maybe that's the price I had to pay for trying to rescue you.'

She curled her trembling fingers into a fist.

'I could have told you nothing, Eve. I could have simply kept driving after letting him know that you were all looking for him. Left you thinking well of me. And maybe I could have come back into your life in the future and had a chance. But here I am instead, destroying any chance of us being together by telling you the hard truth about your brother. So you hear it from me rather than from him.'

Her voice was barely more than a croak. 'What do you mean?'

'I've seen your route maps, Eve.' He sighed. 'You would have reached his town before Christmas. And *you* would have found him drinking in that pub, and *you* would have had to stand there, struggling to be strong as he told you how he'd traded up to a better new life rather than the tough old one he'd left, and as he threw everything you've sacrificed and been through back in your face.'

She reached out for something solid to hold on to and found nothing. Because he wasn't there for her any more.

'And you would have knocked on his door the next morning with takeaway coffee, only to find he'd cleared out, with not a single clue. And you would have spent the rest of your life hunting for him.

'And so, even though it hurts like death to do this to you, I would take this pain one hundred times over to spare you from it.'

She stared at him through glistening eyes—wordless—as he stepped up closer.

'I'm not fool enough to think there's a place for me here now, even if you did have some capacity in your heart. I wouldn't expect—or even want—to just slide into the emotional vacancy left by your brother. Or your mother. Or anyone else you've ever loved.

'I deserve my *own* piece of you, Eve. Just mine. I think that's all I've ever really wanted in my sorry excuse for a life. The tiniest patch of your heart to cultivate with beautiful flowering vines and tend and spoil until they can spread up your walls and through your cracks and over your trellises. Until you've forgotten what it was like to *not* have me there. In the garden of your heart.'

He leaned down and kissed her, careless of the puffy, slimy, tear-ravaged parts of her. Long, hard and deep. A farewell. Eve practically clung to the strong heat of his lips.

'But I can't do anything with the rocky, parched earth you'll have left after all this is over. Nothing will ever grow there.'

He tucked a strand of damp hair behind her ears and murmured, 'Go home, Eve. Put him behind you. Put me behind you. Just…heal.'

This time, he didn't pause at the door, he just pushed through, jumped down to the ground and strode off, leaving Eve numb, trembling and destroyed in the little bus that had become her cage.

CHAPTER THIRTEEN

Five months later

MARSHALL SPRINTED UP the valley side to the cottage, sweaty from a morning of post-hole-digging and dusting the rich dirt off his hands as he went. He snatched the phone up just before his voicemail kicked in.

Landline. Not many people called that any more.

'Hello?'

'Marshall?'

A voice familiar yet…not. Courtesy of the long-distance crackle.

'Yeah. Who's this?'

'Travis Read.'

His heart missed a beat. 'Has something happened?'

That was their agreement. Marshall would call twice a year to check in and, apart from that, Travis would only call if something was up. It had only been five months since they'd last spoken. He wasn't yet due.

'No, I'm…uh…I'm in town this afternoon and wondered if I could come and see you.'

Since Travis only had his new Victorian phone number, not his new home address, 'in town' had to mean Melbourne. That was all the area code would have told him. But what could Eve's brother possibly have to say? And why did he sound so tense? Unless it was recriminations. It occurred to him to question why he would have caught a plane anywhere since that would flag him on the Federal Police's radar and risk exposure. Unless he used a fake name. Or drove. Or maybe his family had taken him off the missing-persons register so that scarce resources weren't wasted on a man who wasn't really missing.

He'd given Travis one more go all those months ago for Eve's sake. Pointlessly tried to get him to change his mind, told him the damage it had done to his own life—in the long-term—to walk away from his family, as imperfect as they were. How it hadn't solved any of his problems at all—he'd just learned to function around them.

Or not, as the case may be.

But Travis hadn't budged. He was as stubborn as his sister, it seemed. And now he wanted to meet.

Irritation bubbled just below Marshall's surface. He was already keeping Travis's secret at the expense of his own happiness. Hadn't he done enough?

But then he remembered how important this kid was to the woman he was still struggling to get over and he reluctantly shared his new address and gave Travis a time later in the day before trundling back down the hill to the Zen meditation of punching three-dozen fenceposts into the unsuspecting earth.

About fifteen minutes before Travis was due, Marshall threw some water on his face and washed his filthy hands. The rest… Travis would have to take him as he found him.

About six minutes after their appointed time Marshall heard a knock at his front door and spied a small hire car out of one of the windows as he reached the door.

'Trav—?'

He stopped dead. Not Travis.

Eve.

In the flesh and smiling nervously on his doorstep.

His first urge was to wrap her up in his arms and never, ever let her go again. But he fought that and let himself frown instead. His quick brain ran through the facts and decided that she was obviously here in Travis's place. Which suggested Eve and Travis were in communication.

Which meant—his sinking heart realised—that everything he'd done, everything he'd given up, counted for absolutely nothing.

'How did you find him?'

'Good to see you, too,' she joked. Pretty wanly. But he wasn't in any mood for levity. Not while he was feeling this ambushed.

'I didn't find him,' she finally offered. 'He found me.'

So Travis had finally found the personal courage to pick up the phone. Good for him.

And—yeah—he'd be a hypocrite if not for the fact that he'd since taken his own advice and done the same with Rick. His brother hadn't commented on the new mobile number but Marshall felt certain he'd tried to use the old one. That was why he'd yanked out the SIM and tossed it somewhere along the Bussell Highway the same awful night he'd last seen Eve.

The whole world could just go screw itself. Travis. Eve. Rick.

Everyone.

'I was heading home,' Eve said now. 'Backtracking through Esperance. My phone rang and I thought it might be you, but…it was him.'

The flatness of her tone belied the enormity of what that moment must have meant for Eve.

'Why would you think it was me?' Hadn't they been pretty clear with each other when they'd parted?

She shrugged lightly. 'I'd tried your number

several times and it was disconnected, but—you know—hope springs eternal.'

On that cryptic remark, she shuffled from left foot to right on his doorstep.

Ugh, idiot. He stepped aside. 'Sorry, come on in.'

There was something about her being here. Here, where he'd had to force himself finally to stop imagining what the cottage would be like with her in it. It felt as if he'd sprinted up the valley side and into an alternate dimension where his dreams had finally turned material.

Inside, she glanced around her and then crossed straight to the full wall window that looked out over the picturesque valley.

'Gorgeous,' she muttered almost to herself.

While she was otherwise occupied with the view, he took the opportunity to look at her. She'd changed, but he couldn't quite put his finger on how. Her hair was shorter and glossier but not that different. Her eyes at the front door had been bright but still essentially held the same wary gaze he remembered. She turned from the window and started to comment further on his view when it hit him. It was the way she carried herself; she seemed…taller. No, not taller—straighter. As if a great burden she'd been carrying around was now gone.

And maybe it was.

But having her here—in his sanctuary—wasn't good for him. It physically hurt to see her in his space, so he cut to the chase and stopped her before she offered some view-related platitude.

'What are you doing here, Eve?'

Maybe she deserved his scepticism. The way they'd left things… Certainly, Eve had known she wouldn't be walking into open arms.

'I'm sorry for the deception,' she began. 'I wasn't sure you'd see me. We didn't really leave things… open…for future contact. Your phone was dead and your infuriating Government privacy procedures meant no one in your department would give me your new one. And you moved, too.'

She caught herself before she revealed even more ways she'd tried to reach out to him. It wasn't as if she'd been short of time.

'Yet here you are.'

'I guilted Travis into hooking this up,' she confessed. 'He wasn't very happy about betraying you when you've kept his secret in good faith.'

Which explained the tension on the phone earlier. And the long-distance hum. 'To absolutely no purpose, it seems, since you two are now talking.'

'"Talking" is probably an overstatement,' she said. 'We speak. Now and again. Just him and me at this stage but maybe Dad in the future. Trav reached out a few months ago. Said you'd called him again.'

'I did.' Though it had never occurred to him that the contents of that call might some day end up in Eve's ear.

'Talking about everything that happened is pretty hard for him,' she said flatly. 'You were right about that. And you were right that he would have bolted if I'd pushed. He was very close to it.'

'That's partly why I called him again. To make sure he hadn't already done a runner.'

But not the only reason. 'Whatever you talked about, Travis got a lot out of it. It was a real turning point for him.'

Silence fell between them and Eve struggled to know how to continue. His nerves only infected her more.

'So, you went home?' Marshall nudged.

'I was paralysed for a few days,' she admitted. 'Terrified of any forward move in case I accidentally ended up in his town and triggered another disappearance. You could hardly tell me which town not to visit, could you?'

She fought the twist of her lips so that it felt more like a grimace. Great—finally tracked him down and she was grinning like the Joker.

'So I backtracked the way I'd come,' she finished. 'That seemed safe.'

'I wondered if you might still be in Western Australia,' he murmured.

So far away. 'There wasn't anything to stay for.'

Travis in lockdown. Marshall gone. Her journey suspended. She'd never felt so lonely and lost.

'So, here you are.'

'Here I am.' She glanced around. 'And here *you* are.'

All these months he'd been here, within a single day's mountain drive of her family home. God, if only she'd known. She would have come much sooner.

'Do you know where we are?' he asked.

Not exactly warm, but not quite hostile. Just very...restrained.

'The satnav says we're near MacKenzie Falls.' A place they'd both enjoyed so much on their separate trips around the country. 'That's quite a coincidence.'

'Not really. It was somewhere I wanted to come back to.'

Okay. Not giving an inch. She supposed she deserved that.

'You gave up meteorology?'

'No. I consult now. From here, mostly. The wonder of remote technology.'

She glanced out at the carnage in his bottom paddock. 'When you're not building fences?'

'Who knew I'd be so suited to farming.'

'I think you could do pretty much anything you turned your hand to.'

'Thanks for the vote of confidence. Now why are we having this conversation, Eve?'

She sighed and crossed closer to him.

'I wanted to… I *need to* thank you.'

'For what?'

Her fingers were frozen despite the warm day. She rubbed the nerves against her jeans. 'The wake-up call.'

He crossed his arms and leaned on his kitchen island. Okay, he wasn't going to make this any easier.

'When you love a missing person,' she started, 'you can't grieve, you can't move on. You can't plan or make life decisions. So it just becomes easier to… not. It hurts less if you just shut down. And when one system goes down, they all do.

'In my case,' she went on, 'I coped by having a clear, single purpose.'

Find Travis.

'And that was all I could deal with. All I could

hold in my head and my heart. I developed tunnel vision.'

Marshall studied the tips of his work boots.

'I once told you that if Travis walked in the door, healthy and alive, nothing he'd done would matter.'

He nodded. Just once.

'Me dealing with it so maturely was every bit as much a fantasy as him walking in the door unannounced. Turns out, I'm not so stoic under pressure.' She lifted her eyes. 'It matters, Marshall. It matters a lot. Even as I argued with people who warned me that he might not be alive, I secretly wanted them to be right. Rather than accept he might torture his family like this, deliberately. Leave us wondering forever. And then I hated myself for allowing those thoughts.'

Realisation dawned on his face. 'So when it turned out to be true...'

She shook her head. 'I'm very sorry for the things I said. The way I said them. I thought you were putting Travis ahead of me and that clawed at my heart. I'm sorry to say it took me days to realise that was what I did to you every single day. Put you second. The truth is, you sacrificed yourself—and any chance of us being together—for me. To help spare me pain.'

'So you came to apologise?'

Could a heart swell under pressure? Because hers felt twice its usual size. Heavy and pendulous and thumpy. And it was getting in the way of her breathing.

'You put yourself second.' After a lifetime of coming second. 'For me. Not many men would have done that.'

His voice, when it came, was not quite steady. But still a fortress wall. 'So you came to say thanks?'

She took a breath. Inside her long sleeves she twisted her fingers. Over and over. 'I came to see if I'm too late.'

Marshall didn't move. 'Too late for what?'

'For that vision you had,' she said on a sad, weak laugh. 'The timber cabin in the forest with the clear pools…and me. And you,' she finished on a rush.

And the making love twice a day part. She'd clung to that image for the many lonely nights since he'd left.

Marshall gave nothing away, simply pushed from the island bench and moved to stare out of his window.

'You stuck with me, Eve,' he admitted. 'I finished my audit and returned to Sydney, assuming that a little time was all I needed to get you out of my system. But months passed and you were still there.

Under my skin like ink. I couldn't shake you. You were wedged in here.'

He tapped his chest with a closed fist.

'But it doesn't really matter what my heart thinks because my head knows better. And if my life has taught me anything, it's to listen to my head.' He turned back to her. 'I've walked away from much longer relationships than ours when they weren't good for me, Eve. Why would I set myself up to be the second most important person in your life?'

'That's not—'

'So, yes, Eve. I got the cottage in the forest sur-rounded by pools and, yes, I hope to be happy here. Very happy.' He expelled a long, sad breath. 'But no…there's no *you* in that plan any more.'

A rock of pain lodged in her stomach.

'At all?' she whispered.

'You don't have room for me, Eve. I'd convinced myself that you'd cast me as some kind of substitute for your brother but I no longer think that's true. I just don't think you have any emotional capacity left. And I deserve better than sorry seconds.'

She struggled to steady her breath. But it was touch and go. Every instinct she had told her to go, to flee back home. Except that when she'd come here she'd really hoped that *this* might turn out to be home.

And no home worth having came without risk. It was time to be brave.

'I wasn't out there to find Travis,' she whispered, taking the chance. 'I think I was out there trying to find a way to let him go.'

She shuddered in a breath. 'But that was terrifying. What if I had nothing but a massive, gaping hole inside where my love and worry and pain for him used to be? What if I could never fill it? Or heal it. Who was I without him? So much of *me* was gone.'

His strong arms wrapped across his chest and all she could think about was wanting them around her.

'And what little was left around the outside was just numb.' She stepped closer to him. 'But then you came in with your ridiculous orange motorbike and your hairy face and your tattoos and you were like… an icebreaker. Shoving your stubborn way through the frost. Inch by inch.'

A tragic kind of light flickered weakly behind his eyes and it sickened her that she'd been the one to extinguish it before. The memory of him standing in her bus, appealing from the heart, in visible, tangible pain. And she'd not been able to feel a thing.

But his body language was giving nothing away now.

'I'm not a plug, Eve. I'm a person. You'll have to find someone else to fill the void.'

'I don't want you to fill it. I want you to bridge it.'

His eyes came up.

Eve picked up a cushion off his sofa and hugged it close. 'When you left, it was horrible. You gone. Travis gone. Mum gone. Dad on the other side of the country. I'd never felt so alone. Which is ridiculous, I realise, given I'd been travelling solo all year.'

His brow twitched with half a frown, so quick she almost missed it. His posture shifted. Straightened. 'What changed?'

'I couldn't stay frozen.' She shrugged. 'I tried to do what I'd done before, just…deal. But all these emotions started bubbling up out of nowhere and I realised that I'd been harbouring the same feelings Travis must have had since Mum died. Despair. Anxiety. I'd been suppressing them, just like he must have.'

'So you developed some empathy for your brother. That's great.'

'I wasn't thinking about him, Marshall,' she rushed to correct. 'God knows, I should have been, and it took me a while to notice, but eventually I thought how strange it was that I should feel such despair about my brother being *alive*. Anger, sure. Resentment, maybe. But despair…?

'Travis has been absent in my life since Mum died. Even back when he was still physically present. I'd learned how to compensate for his absence and not fall apart. But there I was, trundling up the highway, completely unable to manage my feelings about the absence of someone I'd known less than a fortnight.'

His face lifted. His eyes blazed. But he didn't say a word.

'I wasn't thinking about Travis. I wasn't weeping about Travis. I was thinking about you. Missing… you.'

He had nothing to say to that.

'Nothing felt right without you there,' she whispered.

Agony blazed from his tired eyes. 'Do you understand how hard this is to hear? Now?'

It was too late.

Something grasped at her organs and fisted deep in her gut.

She gathered up her handbag. 'I don't want you thinking badly of me, Marshall. I don't want you remembering me as the outback psycho in a bus. I have years' worth of coping mechanisms that I need to unlearn. I barely know where to start. It's going to be a long work in progress.'

She stepped up to him. Determined to get one thing right in their relationship, even if that was goodbye.

'But I'm on my way. Thanks to you. I just didn't

want you never knowing how much you helped me. What a difference you made. I'm just sorry I couldn't return the favour. I'm sorry I hurt you.'

She pushed up onto her toes and pressed a kiss to his face, over the corner of his mouth, and then whispered into it, 'Thank you.'

Then she dropped back onto her soles and turned for the door.

'Eve.'

His voice came just as she slid her hand onto the heritage doorknob. But she didn't turn, she only paused.

'What about that bridge?'

The one over the void where her love for Travis used to be?

'I guess I won't be needing it,' she murmured past the ache in her chest. 'It doesn't go anywhere now.'

He stepped up behind her and turned her to face him. 'Where did it go? Before?'

As she spoke, her eyes moistened and threatened to shame her. But she didn't shy away from it. She was done hiding her emotions.

'Someone once told me about a garden,' she breathed, smiling through the gathering tears. 'One which used to be barren rubble. With old stone walls and handmade trellises, and where someone had planted a beautiful, fragrant vine. That's where it went.'

He swallowed hard. 'How will you visit it with no bridge?'

'I won't,' she choked. 'But I'll imagine it. Every day. And it will grow without me—up and over the trellis, through the cracks in the wall. And eventually it will cover up all the rocky and exposed places where nothing could thrive.'

And then she'd be whole again.

Marshall glanced away, visibly composing himself. And then he spoke. 'There's something you need to see.'

He slid his fingers through hers and led her out through the front door and down the paving stones to the rear of the house where a large timber door blocked the path. He moved her in front of him and reached around her to open the door.

It swung inwards.

And Eve burst into tears.

She stepped through into the garden of her imagination. Complete with trellis, flowering vines, stone wall and even a small fishpond. All of it blurred by the tears streaming down her face.

All so much prettier than she could ever have imagined.

'Don't cry, Eve,' Marshall murmured right behind her. Closer than she'd allowed herself even to dream.

Which only escalated the sobs that racked her uncontrollably.

'It's so perfect,' she squeezed out between gasped breaths.

'I made it for you,' he confessed. 'It was the first thing I started when I came here.'

Her body jerked with weeping. 'Why?'

'Because it's yours—' he shrugged, stroking her hair '—it was always yours.'

He turned her into the circle of his arms. Warm. Hard. Sweaty from a day of work. Heartbreakingly close. One arm pulled her tighter, the other curled up behind her head so that he could press his lips there.

'You are not some outback psycho,' he soothed into her hair. 'You're passionate and warm and you feel things intensely.'

Maybe she could now that the ice inside her was starting to thaw.

'I wanted all that love you kept in reserve for your brother,' he breathed. 'I hated that Travis was hoarding it. That he'd just walked away from it as though it wasn't the most precious commodity on earth.'

She pulled back and gave him a watery smile. 'He doesn't want it.'

'Someone else does, Eve. Every single bit of it.'

Grey eyes blazed down on her. 'I don't care where it comes from, or where it's been. I just care that it's here, in your garden. With me.'

She curled her hands in his shirt. 'You don't hate me?'

'I never hated you,' he soothed. 'I hated myself. I hated the world and everything in my past that stopped me from being able to just love you. And I was angry at myself for trying to be your champion and fix everything, when all I did was make things worse for you.'

'If you hadn't found Travis, I'd still be driving around the country, heartbroken.'

'If I hadn't found Travis, I'd still be driving around with you,' he avowed. 'I would never have left that easily. I would have just given you some breathing space. I was trying to protect you, not control you.'

'I couldn't face the road without you,' she admitted. 'That's why I went home.'

'I have a confession to make,' he murmured. 'This farm wasn't just about MacKenzie Falls. I picked it so that your father wouldn't have to lose you twice.'

She peered up at him and he tackled her tears with his smudged flannel shirt. 'Lose me where?'

'Lose you to here,' he said, kissing one swollen eyelid and then the other. 'To me.'

Breathless tension coiled in her belly. 'You wanted me to come here?'

'I wanted you with me.'

'Five minutes ago you said it was too late.'

'Eve…if I've learned anything from you it's that surviving is not enough. I survived by leaving my mother and brother behind but it didn't change anything—it didn't change me. I've been on emotional hold since then, just like you. And that can work to a point but it's no good forever. At some point I had to take a risk and start believing in people again. In you.'

'I let you down so badly.'

'I was expecting it. I would have found it no matter what.'

Confused joy tripped and fell over its own feet in her mind. 'You believe in me now?'

'Better, Eve. I believe in myself.'

'And you want me to stay here?'

His lips, hot and heavy, grazed hers, and it wasn't nearly enough contact after so long. She chased his touch with her own.

'I want you to *live* here,' he pledged. And then, in case her addled mind really wasn't keeping up, he added, 'With me. And the forest. Somewhere we can retreat to when our crazy all-consuming families get too much. Somewhere we can just be us.'

A joyous blooming began somewhere just behind her heart.

'I'll always worry about him,' she warned. She wasn't simply going to be able to excise Travis from her life the way he'd done to her. Once a big sister, always a big sister.

'I know. And I'll always have the family felon to help keep tabs on him.' Then, at her quizzical expression, he added, 'Long story.'

'Everything I said—'

'*Everything* is in the past, Eve. I'm asking you to choose the future. I'm asking you to choose me.'

The last time he'd asked that of her, she'd chosen her brother. And broken Marshall's soul.

She slid her arms around his gorgeous, hard middle and peered up at him from the heart of their fantasy garden.

'No,' she said breathlessly, and then squeezed him reassuringly as he flinched. 'This time *I choose us.*'

* * * * *

MILLS & BOON®
Large Print – July 2015

THE TAMING OF XANDER STERNE
Carole Mortimer

IN THE BRAZILIAN'S DEBT
Susan Stephens

AT THE COUNT'S BIDDING
Caitlin Crews

THE SHEIKH'S SINFUL SEDUCTION
Dani Collins

THE REAL ROMERO
Cathy Williams

HIS DEFIANT DESERT QUEEN
Jane Porter

PRINCE NADIR'S SECRET HEIR
Michelle Conder

THE RENEGADE BILLIONAIRE
Rebecca Winters

THE PLAYBOY OF ROME
Jennifer Faye

REUNITED WITH HER ITALIAN EX
Lucy Gordon

HER KNIGHT IN THE OUTBACK
Nikki Logan

0615 Rom LP